LEGACY OF FEAR

In a desperate bid to escape the scandal and persecution that follow the unexpected death of her husband, Alicia Cornell flees to the small Cornish town of Poltreath in search of a safe haven. But it soon becomes clear that someone there recognises her — and is intent on blackmail. Suddenly, all the people she knows become suspects. Can it really be one of them? And if so, which one? Is her secret about to be exposed, just when she believed she was safe?

SUSAN UDY

LEGACY OF FEAR

Complete and Unabridged

LINFORD
Leicester

First published in Great Britain in 2020

First Linford Edition
published 2020

A catalogue record for this book is available
from the British Library.

ISBN 978–1–4448–4530–3

1

Time stopped for Petra Matthews as she stared down at the four flat tyres — slashed tyres, she saw upon closer examination, effectively rendering the van impossible to drive.

She gave a moan of despair.

It couldn't all be going to happen again — here — could it? She'd been so sure she'd left this kind of thing behind her; that she was about to start a new life. A life free from fear and intimidation.

But was she maybe overreacting, the shock making her think irrationally? Making her leap to the wrong conclusion entirely? Wasn't it more likely to be a few local youths getting up to mischief? There was little else for them to do here, after all. But as much as she longed to believe that, she couldn't. The damage done was too reminiscent of the things that had happened before. All those awful things that she so desperately wanted to forget.

Before

It was eight thirty on a March morning and Alicia Cornell was preparing to go to work. She was alone in the house. Grant, her husband of ten years, had left earlier to drive to Heathrow to catch a flight to New York. At one time, she would probably have gone with him. Nowadays, she simply didn't have the time. Her own interior decorating business consumed all of her days and a large part of her evenings as well.

But that aside, the truth was she didn't want to accompany him any-more. Their relationship had been struggling for the past couple of years, to the extent that they had begun to occupy separate bedrooms. Nothing had actually been said by either of them, yet somehow they'd drifted into

2

it. Initially, it had been just a couple of nights a week, usually when Grant was going to be returning late; now it was every night.

The truth was, Grant was spending more time abroad. So much so that Alicia felt increasingly excluded from his life. Even when he was in the UK, he seemed incapable of leaving work behind him. The result was Alicia had been inspired to take a plunge into the unknown, launching That Special Touch nine months ago. Since then, she'd acquired a reputation for unusual decorative effects on walls and furnishings, which ensured that commissions were flooding in.

Fifteen years older than her, up until the time she'd started her own business, Grant had been the sole earner. Upon their marriage, it had been his wish that she give up work and devote herself to caring for their home, and initially she'd welcomed that. But as time went by, that pleasure had evaporated and she'd felt the need to be independent; to earn her own money. It had always been her dream to have her own business, and recalling the enthusiasm with which she'd regularly redecorated her bedroom once she was old enough to undertake the task, it seemed a natural progression to enrol on a course in interior decorating and then a further advanced course. A course where she learnt how to achieve various special effects by the use of paint. For instance, transforming a plain stone or wooden fireplace into one that looked like marble; rag rolling a chest of drawers to give a stippled look; patterning a wooden picture frame with a cloth to bestow a soft mottled finish. Her clients had loved it, and the business had expanded way beyond her original ambition. But despite that, she still occasionally longed for the sort of closeness she and Grant had enjoyed at the start of their relationship and throughout the early years of their marriage.

But Grant had become a very

wealthy man; wealthy beyond anything she had aspired to, and lately he'd been spending money in increasing amounts on luxury cars as well as designer clothes, jewellery for himself and her, a villa in the south of France, and a recently acquired apartment in New York — for when he needed to travel there, apparently. He'd even taken on people to help out in their six-bedroom, four-bathroom house. None of which Alicia had wanted.

But it was his latest acquisition, a luxurious yacht, which most concerned her. Apart from the cost of it, she wondered when he'd find the time to enjoy it, especially as they lived miles from the sea. 'It's something I've always wanted,' he'd told her when she quizzed him about it. And when she'd gone on to mention the extent of his spending, asking where the vast amounts of money were coming from, he'd prevaricated and hedged, so she'd given up.

It was true that he'd built up an extensive conglomerate of companies, each operating under the auspices of the parent company, Cornell Enterprises. They consisted of a chain of cafés and coffee bars; he was very proud of the fact that there was one in every major city and town all over the UK. Just after he'd met Alicia, he'd purchased a chain of designer stores, selling everything from clothes to stylish home furnishings. There were also a dozen country house hotels, plus luxury hotels in the south of France, Spain and most recently the US. Added to these was a string of estate agencies, although they were currently struggling in the face of increased online selling.

Alicia had tried to stop worrying, but even so, she noticed the gradual change in him. Over the past three or four months, his air of self-assurance had changed to one of frowning preoccupation. When she finally ventured to ask if something was wrong, he'd turned on her. 'Christ, do you never bloody stop? Nag, nag, nag.' And he'd stormed out of the house.

She sighed now and headed for the front door. Before she could reach it, however, there was a loud knock. She opened it to find two police constables standing there; a man and a woman.

'Hello.' Alicia made no attempt to hide her astonishment. 'Can I help you? If it's my husband you want, he's not here, I'm afraid.'

'We know that, Mrs Cornell.'

Her heart began to thud at that point. The tone of the man's voice was a worrying one.

'What's wrong?' Her breathing quickened, a sensation of dread filling her.

It was the woman PC who now spoke. 'Shall we go inside, Mrs Cornell?'

'Just tell me what's wrong.' Nevertheless, she stood to one side and allowed them in.

It was the man who turned to her once they were in the sitting room. 'I'm very sorry to have to tell you, Mrs Cornell, that your husband has had a serious car accident. He appears to have driven headlong into a large tree. There are no signs of the car going out of control and no evidence of the involvement of any other vehicle. I'm afraid he didn't survive it.'

Alicia stared at him, unable to comprehend what it was she hearing. When she finally recovered her power of speech, all she could stammer was, 'You-you mean you think he committed suicide?'

'It looks very much like it. Obviously we'll investigate further, but it seems pretty clear cut.'

Everything became a blur at that point. She was dimly aware of the female PC making her a cup of tea and then asking if there was someone they could call for her. But everything seemed to be happening somewhere far away. The woman's voice echoed around the room, her words indistinct; barely discernible. Alicia did manage to gather her wits sufficiently to answer, 'No, there's no one.'

'No family?'

Suddenly she was back where she should be, in her own sitting room. She stared at the PC through eyes that were veiled in moisture. She dashed her fingers across them in an attempt to clear her vision. 'Well, y-yes, b-but they're up in Cheshire.' Her words were shaky, wavering. 'And I don't want to . . .'

The truth was, she was reluctant to call her parents, mainly because they barely communicated with her anymore. They and her brother had deeply disliked as well as distrusted Grant, and he'd made no secret of his contempt for them and their modest lifestyles. In return, they had declared that she must have lost her mind. He was far too old for her.

Grant had been in the north for a conference. Alicia had been working in the hotel he'd stayed at, where she'd been training to be a receptionist. She'd been completely bowled over by the handsome businessman. He'd asked her out on the first evening, and the rest

9

was history as they say. He'd travelled up from his home in Worcestershire to see her every weekend after that, and before too long, she'd fallen headlong in love. So when a mere two months after their first meeting he'd asked her to marry him, she'd had no hesitation in agreeing — to her family's vociferous and furious disapproval. She'd been just twenty at the time.

The PCs eventually left her at her request. 'I'd like to be alone, if you don't mind.'

But strangely, once she was, her main emotion, now that her sense of shock had faded, was one of, well — relief. But her shame at that was soon submerged beneath intense anxiety about what she'd do now. About what would happen to Grant's business empire. She wasn't capable of overseeing it. All right, he'd employed the appropriate staff to assist him, but it had been Grant who was the driving force, the linchpin. There was also a hefty mortgage on their house, and

— oh, good Lord, he'd put the house and its contents into her name for tax reasons. She'd now be responsible for maintaining those payments. How would she do that? She had no idea how much money Grant had; accessible money. And would she even be able to draw on it? Panic quickened her heartbeat until it seemed to be pulsating right through her.

It wasn't long, though, before she was made agonisingly aware of the reason for his recent look of preoccupied anxiety. He was suspected of plundering the pensions of his hundreds of employees in order to fund their lavish lifestyle. The fraud office had embarked upon the process of investigating him, so not surprisingly, his various bank accounts were frozen. Apparently he'd hidden the bulk of his fortune in some far-away tax haven, and they were trying to trace it. So far they hadn't been able to find it. Could she help? they asked. Of course she couldn't. What the hell was she to do?

Would she be implicated in his fraud? Panic once again swamped her, this time about possible prosecution.

How could she have been so blindly trusting? Why hadn't she questioned him more? The simple act of transferring the house into her name should have rung alarm bells. As should his moodiness and anger at her questions.

With the story making all the papers, local and national, as well as the TV news, his name was blackened and vilified as more and more emerged of his fraudulent financial activities. He hadn't been making the company pension contributions for any of his employees, and hadn't been for some time. Her name swiftly became tarnished alongside his, and soon reporters turned up on her doorstep, ringing the doorbell, shouting through the letterbox, banging on the door and the windows. 'Did you know what your husband was doing? Were you complicit in it?'

Grant had wanted eight-foot-high

gates at the end of the driveway, but she'd resisted that, declaring such a barrier would make it feel like living in Fort Knox. Now she wished she'd listened to him.

But the truth was, Grant had become a prominent and well-known business-man. He'd appeared several times on *BBC Breakfast* discussing the UK economy. He'd been regarded as a highly successful and much-respected businessman; an entrepreneur, even. He'd been described more than once as the sort of man this country needed.

All Alicia could do was refuse to give any interviews, which meant not leaving the house for fear of being forced to run the gauntlet of press and TV reporters, and putting her business commitments on hold.

His death did result in her mother contacting her, but when, almost at once, she began to angrily voice her criticisms of Grant rather than offering her daughter any help or sympathy, Alicia hung up on her and promptly burst into tears.

It was then that small groups of people began to congregate, adding to the crowd of reporters. Just a few at first, shouting, 'Thief, thief. You must have known what was happening. You've stolen our future. Give us our money back.'

That was bad enough. But then, a couple of evenings later, Alicia was in the sitting room trying to distract herself by watching TV when a brick flew through the window, smashing the glass and missing her by mere inches. She leapt from her armchair to gingerly pick her way through the broken fragments to the window, peering out to see a dozen or so people standing just feet away from the house. They spotted her and began shouting again, at the same time shaking their fists.

She lurched backwards and grabbed her phone, intending to call the police, before realising the shouting had stopped. For a second time, she peered out of the window. There was no one there. Hoping it was just a one-off incident, she decided not to bother the police with it and instead went to fetch a pan and brush. She had no help in the house nowadays. She couldn't afford it, she'd reasoned, but apart from that she didn't want people around her, not even people she'd grown to know well. She'd noticed the looks they'd given her as they went about their chores. So it was a relief when one morning they didn't turn up.

It was at that point that things began to get very much worse than staff leaving and bricks being thrown. Her car tyres were slashed; she'd left Grant's cars in the garage so they weren't attacked. She resolved to do the same with hers the next night, after she'd had the tyres replaced with new ones. There was plenty of room. Then the words 'Pension thief' were painted on the garage doors in foot-high red letters. A couple of nights after that, Alicia's precious plants were uprooted in the front garden and strewn around, ensuring that most of them were dead by morning. Fortunately a high gate, which Grant had insisted upon and which they'd always kept locked, and brick walls barred entrance to the rear of the house. On another night, her dustbin was emptied all over the drive, and on one awful occasion dog poo was pushed through the letterbox. Each time, she notified the police, but they seemed powerless to stop it. Not surprisingly, Alicia became stressed almost beyond endurance.

She dreamed of people outside the house, surrounding it, watching her, but whenever she got out of bed to look there was no one there. Sleep constantly eluded her. Instead, at the slightest sound, she'd stand at the bedroom window, staring into the shadows, straining to see if anyone was out there.

Things did eventually calm down. She'd tried ringing her parents, hoping to make peace between the three of them, but upon having the phone put down on her each time she did, she gave up on that too. She felt alone and abandoned. She even tried calling her brother Paul, but all he would say was, 'I don't wish to be associated in any way with you or your despicable husband. I've never liked him, but this — I can't believe you didn't know.'

When she protested that she'd had nothing to do with what he'd done, all he said was, 'Really? Didn't you ever question his enormous level of spending? Ask where the money was coming from? Are you that naive? Don't ring me again.'

And finally, one by one, her friends deserted her. Clients cancelled their commissions, clearly not wanting the wife of a criminal in their houses. Thankfully, the police and the fraud investigators believed her when she insisted she'd known nothing of Grant's activities, and cleared her of any wrongdoing.

So with his cremation well behind her — a largely unnoticed affair by anyone other than her, Grant having no family to speak of, and the final verdict being that he had committed suicide — she concluded there was no reason for her to stay in the area. She'd been the target of everyone's hate and vilification for long enough. She'd move to somewhere where no one would know her. The only drawback to that was the fact that both her name and her face were known all over the country. To add to her troubles, the mortgage company had been making noises about the repossession of the house. She hadn't been able to make any payments and it turned out that Grant hadn't been paying them either. She still had her own money, not a huge amount, but enough to live on for a couple of months at least. Any money in Grant's bank accounts had been seized.

For it turned out that he'd also been consistently falsifying company accounts, as well as extracting large sums of money. This, along with plundering the employees' pensions, meant the companies were all found to be insolvent. The group as a whole began collapsing into bankruptcy. This was followed very quickly by both the villa in France and the New York apartment being repossessed. They'd both been mortgaged as well. Things couldn't get any worse.

Determined to put it all behind her, Alicia began making preparations to leave. She'd go somewhere where no one would know her, hopefully. She rather fancied Cornwall, so she went online and found a small fully furnished cottage on the south coast to rent. Surely no one would know her there.

She managed to sell some of the furniture, which added a respectable sum to her bank account. The items that no one wanted, she donated to various charities. As for the cars, hers included, they'd all been leased, and, as it turned out, so had the yacht. They were all returned to the leasing companies. She used some of her money to buy herself a used VW Polo hatchback. She would hand in the house keys to the mortgage company as she left the village. Suddenly, she felt the weight she'd been labouring under diminish. A fresh beginning. That was what she wanted.

As a precaution against recognition, she dyed her hair, turning honey blonde into warm chestnut, and then had it cut, shortening its middle-of the-back length to a just-above-the-shoulder bob.

She used coloured contact lenses — you could get anything online these days — to change her blue eyes to brown. The extreme stress she'd been under meant she'd lost weight, thinning her face to reveal its delicate bone structure. Finally, she changed her name by deed poll, a very quick process if done online. She became Petra Matthews, Petra being her rarely used middle name and Matthews her mother's maiden name. No one would recognise that.

So, with all of her preparations

complete, she set about packing everything she could into the back of her small car. Amongst the items was her jewellery, even though Grant had bought most of it, the reason being she'd be able to sell it if she needed to. She'd certainly never wear it again. Much, much worse than losing the house and its contents was the fact that she'd lost her precious business.

She limited her clothes to jeans and cropped trousers, T-shirts and sweaters, as well as a couple of jackets. The rest, mostly designer outfits, went to charity shops. She wouldn't need such garments where she was going. She did take the silver-backed hairbrush set her grandmother had bought her for her eighteenth birthday, and an antique clock that she loved. She also carefully packed several ornaments which she hoped would induce a feeling of home for her, plus a couple of paintings Grant had bought not long before he died, and which she was extremely fond of. They weren't worth a lot, but Grant had believed their value would increase as the artist acquired a reputation. Then, of course, there was her laptop and printer, plus a box full of her favourite books, and lastly a couple of photograph albums, mainly of her brother and her parents during their childhood and teenage years. She burnt the rest.

The house she'd rented was a two-bedroom cottage in the small town of Poltreath. Its name was Sea View Cottage — a bit of a misnomer, Petra discovered when she got there. It was perched on the summit of a hill, but even so, you could only glimpse a sliver of blue water from one of the bedrooms. Tall trees partially blocked the view, bordering the cliff top a hundred yards or so away. Still, they would offer some protection from the winds that would almost certainly blow straight off the sea.

The room with the view, although not much more than a single room, could be the spare room. Any guests that came could have hers. It was a larger room and looked out over the road and onto fields that stretched away on the other side. However, sea view or not, the cottage itself looked comfortable. It consisted of a medium-sized fitted kitchen, a comfortable sitting room with a log burner around which was grouped a three-seater settee, and two armchairs. There was a television, a bookcase crammed with paperbacks, a coffee table and a bureau. Although there was no dining room, the kitchen contained a small round table and two chairs. From a dinky entrance hall a flight of stairs climbed steeply to the two bedrooms. Next door to the main bedroom was the one and only bathroom, which was perfectly adequate for her. There were also two large storage cupboards alongside, one of which contained bedding and towels. That would be useful until she could get round to buying her own.

But the most appealing feature to her

was that the cottage was situated on its own, the nearest house being out of sight and over another hill. An added bonus was the fact that the town itself was a good fifteen-minute walk away, and then only if you walked quickly. The nearest beach, the estate agent had informed her when she picked up the door key, was a seven- or eight-minute walk in the opposite direction to the town. The road petered out there apparently, and all that lay beyond was acres of countryside. A clifftop walk began at that point as well. 'The path up is a bit steep and rough,' he'd told her, 'but the views once you're there are well worth the climb.'

As for the town itself, she'd driven through it to get to the cottage and, as far as she could tell, it consisted of a fairly large quay with various boats and yachts moored alongside, and a main street, Fore Street, which ran in a straight line from one end of the town to the other. The shops that lined both sides of this were mostly fancy goods shops, but she'd noted a Spar, a bakery, a butcher, a greengrocer, and a paper shop which, from the sign outside, contained a post office as well. There was even an art gallery with a sign that advertised materials for sale. She'd managed to spot the owner's name above the door, Deborah Harris. There was also a dress and shoe shop. All of which meant she would be able to do most of her shopping locally. Anything she couldn't obtain that way, she'd order online. She'd brought enough food with her to last a couple of weeks at least, three if she was frugal.

So for those first three weeks she lived quietly, avoiding the town and its inhabitants. Instead, she explored the high-hedged lanes with their bounty of wild flowers, mainly primroses and bluebells studded with spikes of pink campion, and traced public footpaths through fields and woods. All of which meant she lost even more weight. Her clothes were beginning to hang on her. But reassuringly, the few people she encountered on her ramblings exhibited no sign of recognition other than to wish her a friendly 'Good day'; and so, gradually, the feelings of strain and fear that had plagued her for weeks eased.

Nonetheless, the first time she decided to venture into town, she couldn't suppress her anxiety. But the walk swiftly banished her fears; no one gave her a second glance.

As it was the beginning of May, the sun was blazing from a speedwell-blue sky. Trees, interspersed with houses the closer she got to the town itself, lined both sides of the road, disappearing almost completely as she entered the town, allowing her gaze to reach out over the water to the small town on the other side of the estuary. The water's surface sparkled in the morning sunshine. Seagulls swooped and screeched as a fishing boat came in, and she spotted what she thought was a cormorant flying low, its wings almost touching the water as it headed upriver. As if to put the finishing touch to this idyllic scene, several yachts zigzagged across the surface, their sails billowing and flapping in the brisk morning breeze.

Her first port of call was the butcher's shop. The rosy-cheeked man who stood behind the counter smiled warmly at her and asked, 'And what can I do for you, my dear?'

Such was her pleasure in this display of geniality that she grinned back, equally as warmly, before giving him her order. She received the same friendly greeting wherever she went. It reinforced her belief that all was going to be well. She'd be safe here from the sort of persecution she'd been on the receiving end of in Compton Green.

The last shop she went to was the bakery, the smell of freshly cooked pasties proving irresistible. As was the smile on the face of the young woman who greeted her arrival with a friendly 'Good morning. How can I help you?'

'I'll have a loaf, please, wholemeal,

and one of your delicious-smelling pasties.'

'Certainly.' The young woman bagged her order and handed it to her over the counter. 'Are you here on holiday, then?'

Petra hesitated. 'No. I-I'm living here.'

'Are you?' The woman's eyebrows lifted in surprise. 'How long have you been here? I've not seen you before.'

'Not long. I haven't been into the town very often.' She didn't say that she'd never been in. The woman might think her odd, and she didn't want to arouse anyone's curiosity.

'So how do you like our little town?'

'So far, so good.' Petra smiled at her.

'Are you here to stay?'

Clearly, there was to be no standing on ceremony. She hid another smile. 'That's the plan.'

'Well, I'm Jenny Graham.' And she held out a hand for Petra to grasp.

'I'm Petra Matthews.'

'You'll have to come into town more often. Where are you living?'

'At Sea View Cottage. I'm renting for the moment.'

Oh, right. 'Are you here with family?'

Good grief, if everyone was as nosey as this woman, she'd have to be cautious. One careless word and her cover would be smashed to smithereens. 'No, I'm alone.'

Jenny frowned. 'It's a bit isolated for someone on their own. Especially a woman.' Curiosity replaced the frown.

'I like it that way.' Petra knew she was sounding curt now, but she couldn't help herself.

'Huh! Just as well. It's okay while it's summertime, but I wouldn't want to be stuck out there in the middle of winter. The gales don't half blow in at that point — straight off the sea. It's brought more than one tree down. Anyway . . . ' Jenny tilted her head to one side as she grinned. It gave her the look of a mischievous child. ' . . . as I said, you'll have to come into town more often. Get to know people. You'll be very welcome. We're a friendly bunch.' If she had taken offence at Petra's curtness, she seemed to have got over it.

The doorbell chimed as someone else entered the shop.

'Ah, Isobel,' Jenny greeted the woman who'd come in, 'you're just in time to meet our newest resident, Petra Matthews. She's living out at Sea View — on her own.' She lifted an eyebrow at the other woman.

Petra met the gaze of a plump middle-aged woman.

'Hello.' She held out a hand. 'I'm Isabel Pearce. Nice to meet you. I'm always pleased when a fresh face joins our community. But — Sea View.' She pulled a face. 'Bit isolated, isn't it?'

Was everyone going to make a big thing of that? Petra grimly wondered. 'It suits me, as I told Jenny.'

The woman shrugged. 'Well, each to their own. Anyhow, if you're interested or want some company, we have lots of activities going on that you can join in with, and we're always glad of some fresh blood.' She smiled warmly. 'I'm a member of a painting group. We meet every Thursday evening in an upstairs room at the art gallery. If you're interested, it's just a dozen or so of us. There's also a drama society if you're into acting.'

'I don't think so,' Petra said. She was acting a part all the time as it was. That was more than enough to contend with. Especially when she was so acutely aware that one heedless word could reveal her identity. But the art group, painting on canvas rather than walls, that was something she'd always wanted to do. And who knew, maybe if she resurrected her business she could eventually turn her hand to painting murals. 'But the art group is a possibility.'

'In that case, do come along. We meet at six thirty. Debs, the gallery owner, sets it all up for us. We're working on a still life at the moment. She also gives great advice, being an artist herself.'

31

'I'll think about it,' Petra murmured. She didn't want to commit herself until she'd had time to consider it a little bit more. 'Maybe in another week or so. I'm still settling in.'

'You'll be very welcome. Actually, I live not too far from you. You'd have passed me. Number 43, on the left. Handy for the shops. Bit more sheltered than your place, too. Maybe you'd like to pop in sometime for a cuppa?'

'I'd like that,' Petra said.

'I've got my daughter and teenage granddaughter living with me at the moment, which is nice. I'm on my own — ' Her expression darkened momentarily. ' — so it's company.'

Petra left the shop feeling as if she'd just been put through some form of inquisition. These small towns could be hotbeds of gossip. Compton Green had been the same. Everyone knew everyone else, and secrets didn't stay that way for long, as she'd discovered to her cost.

She was deep in thought as she

prepared to cross the road to a café she'd noticed. She intended treating herself to a coffee and maybe a scone and cream, a reward for her courage in venturing into town. She had one foot already in the road when a silver-grey Jaguar swept by, practically brushing her as it did so. She jerked backwards, only just managing to save herself from falling, but, even so, she caught a glimpse of the driver. He was staring through his side window at her, eyes like grey pebbles. She glared back at him. He was driving far too fast for such a narrow road. There were pedestrians and children everywhere. Any of them could have walked in front of his car. Despite her anger, though, she managed to spot that he was an incredibly handsome man, with chiselled features and high cheekbones above a steely jawline. She wondered who he was.

She didn't have to wonder long, however, because a familiar voice spoke from right behind her. It was Jenny, from the bakery.

'I see you've noticed our most handsome and richest resident, the notorious Finn Hogarth.'

'He might be rich and handsome, but he's also arrogant and dangerous. Imagine driving along a street like this in such a careless fashion. It's a wonder he hasn't killed someone.'

'Ooh.' Jenny laughed. 'Don't let anyone else hear you saying all that. He's regarded as practically a god round here, at least by the majority of the women.'

Petra snorted. 'Really? Some god. He'd have no compunction in mowing one of them down, I'm sure, if they got in his way.'

'Wow! You've really taken a dislike to him, haven't you?'

'Well, as he almost knocked me down — yes.'

'Lord, did he?'

Petra nodded. 'He didn't even have the grace to stop and apologise. He quite clearly blamed me.' Although, to be fair, she had practically walked in front of him, so maybe he'd had some justification for his glaring look.

'Well, I think you need a cup of coffee.' Jenny indicated the café just ahead of them. 'I could join you if you don't mind.' She raised a quizzical eyebrow. 'I'm having an early lunch break. I like someone to chat to, someone who isn't simply buying bread from me that is.' And she gave another cheeky grin.

As for Petra, she wasn't sure she wanted company right at this moment, but as it would seem rude to say no and the last thing she wanted was to upset anyone this soon after her arrival, she acquiesced with a smile.

But she soon found herself wondering whether she'd made a huge miscalculation. Because the second they were seated with their cappuccino coffees in front of them, Jenny wasted no time in asking, 'So — tell me all about yourself. What do you do?'

2

Petra's response was a short one. 'Nothing at the moment.'

'Oh?' Jenny again raised an eyebrow, but undaunted by Petra's curt tone, went on, 'So how do you plan to pass the time, then? As picturesque as Poltreath is, it's not exactly the centre of the universe, and its nightlife is practically non-existent — well, apart from the pubs, that is, and they can be pretty lively at times.'

Petra regarded her. She was an attractive woman with her blue eyes, freckled nose and auburn hair. She wasn't tall, five feet two or three, Petra estimated, but she was curvy; the sort of woman that men gazed at admiringly.

Petra felt a pang of envy. She'd always considered her own breasts too small, even though they measured a respectable thirty-six inches and were perfectly in proportion to her twenty-six-inch waist and thirty-seven-inch hips.

Feeling she needed to say something to justify her existence, as well as make herself sound less uninteresting, she said, 'I did have my own interior decorating business.'

'Did you? Where was that?'

It was the question she'd been dreading. The name Compton Green had been mentioned in every newspaper report at the time, and she couldn't be sure that people wouldn't remember it. She deliberately made her response a vague one. 'Worcestershire.'

But she wasn't to be let off that lightly. 'Where in Worcestershire?'

'Oh, y-you wouldn't know it,' she prevaricated. 'It's no-not much more than a hamlet, really.'

'So, what made you leave a business behind and come here?'

'I-I fancied a change. My husband died.'

Her words did exactly what she'd hoped they would do. They distracted Jenny from the question of where she'd come from.

'Oh, I'm so sorry. Actually, I've just ended things with my partner. Well, to be truthful, he was the one to end it. He decided he preferred someone with a model's figure. Had an aversion, he suddenly informed me, to fat women.' She pulled a comical face, but Petra easily discerned her hurt.

'You're not fat. You have a very nice figure.'

Honestly, what was it with these men? They were never satisfied with what they'd got. She'd wondered more than once whether Grant was having an affair — or maybe affairs.

'Thanks,' Jenny said. 'So what are you going to do here, then?'

'I was thinking of getting my business going again. I specialized in unusual finishes, two of which are a marbling effect using paint, and a process called frottage; it creates the look of ancient parchment on walls. It's really gorgeous and different. I can also offer rag rolling, sponging, stippling — a wide variety of finishes, in fact. Would something like that do well here, do you think? Or is everyone a DIY enthusiast?'

'Some are, some aren't. I'd imagine you'd do pretty well. There are a lot of wealthy retired folk here and I can't imagine they'd want to do their own decorating. People like Finn Hogarth's parents, for example.'

'Yeah, going back to him. Why is he so worshipped here? He looked pretty ordinary to me.'

'Ordinary?' Jenny scoffed. 'Are you blind? The man's bloody gorgeous. And as rich as Croesus, to boot. All by the age of thirty-eight.'

Petra made no comment in response to that statement. She was only too aware that wealth didn't automatically bring happiness in its wake. Mere riches would never count with her. Kindness, consideration for others, tenderness were much more important qualities in her opinion. Nonetheless, she couldn't help asking, 'Married?'

'No, never has been. In fact, he's got himself a reputation as a bit of a ladies' man. And who can blame him? He has his pick of women, so ... ' She shrugged. 'After all, why tie yourself to just one woman when you can have a variety? But be warned. More than a few have had their hearts broken.'

'I'll steer well clear, then. He sounds like the last thing I need at the moment.' She decided it was time to change the subject. 'What does everyone do round here, then?'

'Oh, this and that. As Isabel said, there's an art club you could join. Hey, you'd be good at that, wouldn't you? You being a painter and all.' And Jenny laughed.

It was an infectious sound and had Petra grinning back at her. 'Not that sort of painter, as you well know.'

'Well, it's all the same in my book.' And Jenny laughed again. 'No offence.

You should join them. And talking of books, there's a book club, too. You're told which book to read and then you all get together once a month in the Galleon and discuss it. Although from what I've heard, it's more like an opportunity to have a few glasses of wine. There's the Am Dram society; the Poltreath Players to give them their rightful title. Isobel's a member of that, too. Mind you — ' Jenny gave an arch smile. ' — from what I've heard recently, the poor woman needs to get out now and again.'

'Oh, why's that?'

'That granddaughter of hers, Tara. She's fifteen and a bit of a handful, apparently. As is her daughter, Sally.' She paused as if unsure whether to continue or not. 'Well, I may as well tell you — you'll probably hear it all on the grapevine — Sally's suffering a quite severe bout of depression. Her latest relationship fell apart, just one of many, or so I've heard. She had Tara at eighteen, and I don't think she's even sure who the father is.' Jenny raised her eyebrows. 'A bit of a goer by all accounts, though you'd never hear Isobel say that. Anyway, they both decided to move in with Isobel. But it isn't only that that the poor woman has to contend with.' Again, she paused. 'Tom, her husband, has vanished.'

'Oh no,' Petra cried. 'When?'

'It must be five, six weeks ago. He discovered he'd lost a large part of his pension. Do you remember that case? February, I think it was, when it all came to light. Grant somebody or other. He didn't pay his contributions into the pension scheme for his employees just so he could live like a king. Him and that wife of his. He also falsified his company accounts, grabbing even more money for himself.' Jenny snorted contemptuously. 'The wife says she didn't know what he was doing. Lying bitch — she must have known. Anyway, Tom worked at one of his hotels in Bodmin. Something managerial, I believe. Of course, it eventually closed in the wake of the scandal, so he was out of work as well as losing most of his pension. They reckon he had some sort of mental breakdown, and he simply walked out of the house and didn't come back.'

Petra couldn't speak. She was far too engaged in keeping her expression blank.

'I'm not surprised the thieving bastard killed himself. Mind you, people are beginning to wonder whether Tom's done the same, you know — killed himself. Isobel's been in a dreadful state. Although talking to her, you wouldn't know it. But you don't get over a thing like that, do you? I think that's why she keeps herself so busy.'

Still Petra couldn't speak.

'Are you okay?' Jenny was watching her intently, her brow creased in a frown. 'Oh Lord, he didn't do the same to you, did he? Is that why you moved here?'

'Oh, no.'

'Your husband then?'

'No; as I said, he-he died. He hadn't been well for a while.'

'Right. Well, they've had photos of Tom all over local TV and the papers, but there have been no sightings of him.'

'I'm so sorry,' Petra murmured.

'Yeah, we all are. We all try and do our bit to help, but Isobel's a very proud woman and won't accept charity. In fact, she can be a bit prickly at times, between you and me.'

Well, Petra decided, she'd been spot on about the gossip in this place. Was there anything Jenny didn't know about Isobel and her family? Her stomach clenched as her pulse raced. One wrong word and her story would be out there for everyone to pick over. She gnawed at her lower lip. Had she made a huge mistake? Would it have been better to move to a city instead of a small town? She'd have been just one face amongst tens of thousands.

Belatedly, she realised Jenny was staring at her.

44

'I'd swear I've seen you somewhere before. Have you been here on holiday?'

This was exactly what she'd feared — that someone would partially recognise her and start asking questions. Still, at least Jenny had provided her with the perfect get-out. Had she been here on holiday? So, as much as she hated being forced to actually lie rather than simply prevaricate, she said, 'Once or twice, yes. With my husband.'

'Did you stay here in Poltreath?'

Petra hesitated then. If she said yes, Jenny would ask where, and she didn't want to be forced to name a specific location. She wasn't all that familiar with the town yet, so she'd be stuck for an answer if Jenny asked any detailed questions. It seemed best to say, 'No, just outside.'

'Oh, where?'

And that question posed the same problem. She didn't know the surrounding area well enough either, certainly not well enough to be quizzed about it. She took refuge in ambiguity.

'Oh, good Lord. Do you know I can't even remember the name.' She held her breath, pretending to give the matter some thought. She shook her head and gave an apologetic smile. 'No, sorry. It was several years ago, and with all that's happened . . . ' Her smile this time was shaky. 'My husband being so ill.'

'Of course. Sorry. It's my biggest failing. Nosiness. That was something else the boyfriend didn't like.' Her gaze narrowed. 'Still, I could swear . . . '

Petra held her breath. It proved how much on her guard she'd need to be. It also meant that her disguise was nowhere near as effective as she'd believed.

'Well . . . ' Jenny gulped down the last of her coffee. 'I need to get back.'

Struggling to hide her relief, Petra could only muster a weak smile. 'It's been nice meeting you. Um, I've forgotten, what was your surname? Sorry.'

'Graham.'

'Yes, of course. So do you work full

time at the bakery?'

'Yeah. I'm manageress, actually. Of this shop and one in St. Perrin. Although I'm mainly at this one.'

'You've done well then for . . . How old are you? Oh dear, that's a bit rude.'

'That's okay. I'm twenty-five. We must be about the same age?'

'I'm thirty — well, nearing thirty-one, actually.'

'Not much of a gap, then. So how about we get together for an evening and have a drink? Maybe a bite to eat in one of the pubs. The Ship's very good. I could introduce you to a few people.'

'Well, I don't . . . ' Could she bear an entire evening of having to possibly answer yet more probing questions?

'Oh, come on. You can't be a recluse. Everyone will think you're odd.' She gave a provocative grin. 'We're very friendly, so you needn't worry. We stopped smuggling and wrecking a while ago.'

She was right, Petra decided. She couldn't have people wondering what was wrong with her. Or worse, what she might be hiding. 'Okay. When?'

'Tomorrow — Wednesday?'

Despite her doubts, and the fact that she was feeling distinctly steamrollered, she agreed. 'Okay. The Ship?' If she forced herself to go out and about, local people would quickly get used to her face and think nothing of it if someone mentioned they'd seen her before.

'Yeah. Seven thirty?'

'You're on.'

* * *

By the next morning, she felt her confidence growing. She was beginning to make friends, she hadn't made any damaging slips, and she'd been invited out. If she could also get her business going again? Talking about it with Jenny had inspired her to give it a try. She had to do something because she would soon need to start earning money. She had adequate funds for now, but they wouldn't last indefinitely. And besides, running a business would give her something else to think about, to plan.

She would need a new name, though. She couldn't risk using the original one, That Special Touch. Someone might recall it from newspaper reports at the time and put two and two together. She pondered the question for some time. Keep it simple, she finally decided. Petra Matthews, Specialist Interior Finishes. Then, before she could have second thoughts, she designed and produced some simple business cards on her laptop printer, listing just a few of the special effects she could offer along with her mobile and landline phone numbers, plus her email and house address. She only printed fifty to begin with, just to see how it went. Luckily, she'd brought the materials she'd need with her, and she'd done it herself initially, so knew how to go about it. She'd distribute them around the local shops. In fact, she'd go now. One could never be too keen when it came to business.

And so, twenty minutes later, Jenny had agreed to take half a dozen, as had the butcher, along with several of the other shops in Fore Street. She'd naturally had to answer a stream of questions, but she'd expected that and so had her answers prepared. She ended up in the art gallery where the owner, Deborah Harris, showed an encouraging amount of interest.

'It's something this town lacks,' she told Petra. 'A good, innovative decorator with a few new ideas.' She then held out a hand to Petra. 'I'm Deborah — better known as Debs — Harris. I can put you in touch with someone straight away. David and Elizabeth Hogarth.'

Petra frowned. 'Do they have a son, Finn?'

'That's them. Do you know them?'

'No. But I glimpsed him driving through town yesterday. I stepped off the pavement, almost straight into his car.'

'Oh, dear.' Debs pulled a face. 'I bet

that didn't go down well.'

'It didn't. His expression would have frozen hot water.'

'I can imagine.' Debs was regarding her keenly now. 'So how long have you been here? I haven't seen you before.'

Which meant Petra was forced to once again supply what information she could without giving too much away. She was becoming more confident in supplying the details, such as they were. Mind you, she had repeated them a few times now, so she was well rehearsed. Yet again, the loneliness of the cottage was remarked on, and once again she said, 'I like it that way.'

Finally, Debs said, 'I'll give you the Hogarths' phone number and I'll make sure they get one of your cards. Elizabeth was only asking me the other day if I knew of a decorator with a bit of imagination. She said she needs several rooms redone.'

'Thank you so much,' Petra replied with heartfelt gratitude.

'Now then, on the same sort of

subject, can I interest you in buying a painting?'

'Not just at the moment, but I am thinking of joining your art class so I'll need paints, brushes, et cetera.'

'Of course. If you'd like to come with me.' She steered Petra into a small side room. It was stacked with everything she imagined she'd need.

'Oh, that's great. I'll be back when and if I decide to join you all. I love your paintings, by the way.' She indicated the many examples hanging on the walls. 'Did you paint them all?'

'Oh, good grief, no. Mine are the oils; the rest I have here on a sale or return basis. All local artists.'

'Well, I'll certainly have a better look another time. The walls of the cottage could do with brightening up.'

'I'll look forward to that, then. And it's very good to meet you.' Again she proffered a hand. 'Hopefully I'll see you one of the Thursdays, if not before.'

Petra glanced back at her as she

headed for the door. 'Actually, I'm going to the Ship this evening to meet Jenny Graham.'

'Oh, I know Jenny very well. If you wouldn't mind, and I don't think she would, I'd love to join you both. I could do with an evening out. And I'd really like to get to know you.'

'That would be great. I'll look forward to it. Seven thirty, okay?'

She set off for home again, well pleased with the way her day had gone. Debs had even been able to give her the name of a supplier of at least some of the materials she'd need to get her business off the ground. She was sure she'd find more online. Everything was falling into place.

However, by the time six thirty came round and she began to get ready to go out, her confidence was once more on the wane. What on earth would these new friends think of her if they ever discovered the truth? Would they assume that she had connived in Grant's fraudulent activities? Or been complicit, at the very least, as Jenny had?

It was enough to make her glance down over her cream linen cropped trousers and denim jacket and wonder whether she should take them off again, slip into her pyjamas, and stay at home in front of the television. But then, what would Debs and Jenny think when she failed to turn up? And would word get round that she was unreliable? That wouldn't help her start a business.

And after all she'd been through, didn't she owe it to herself to forge a new beginning?

With her confidence at least partly restored, she finished putting on her makeup. She brushed her shoulder-length bob, optimistically pinning several strands up onto the top of her head, before finishing off with a generous application of hair lacquer. The trouble was that whatever she did with it, her hair refused to co-operate, and before she knew it, would have worked its way free of the pins, leaving a tangled mess behind.

So there she was, telling herself to disregard her belated misgivings, leaving the house just after seven fifteen. It was a perfect May evening, and it wouldn't take her much longer than twenty minutes or so to walk to the Ship, fifteen if she got a move on. She didn't want to be the first one there, and knowing no one, be forced to sit alone, waiting for the other two. People would stare, and who knew what might happen then? They might begin to wonder who she was, leading them to look harder.

Despite her see-sawing emotions, she set off, and with impeccable timing arrived at the pub a few minutes after seven thirty. To her relief, both Jenny and Debs were there, seated at a table in the window that overlooked the quay and the estuary beyond. A bottle of white wine was already in front of them, along with three wine glasses. To Petra's dismay, though, a man was with them. A fairly nice-looking man, it had to be said, with darkish blond hair, fairly long at the back but starting to recede at the temples. He had pale blue deep-set eyes, a long nose and thin lips. He was nursing a pint glass of beer. Still, would have preferred it to be just the three of them.

'Hey, Petra, over here,' Jenny called.

Petra walked across, acutely aware of the many gazes fixed upon her. Surprisingly — it was only seven thirty, after all — the pub was practically full. She felt yet another stab of misgiving as well as the warmth of a blush as she reached the table. She'd always hated being the focus of people's attention, but since Grant's arrest she was even more sensitive about it.

Driving all of that out of her mind, she rearranged her expression into what she hoped was one of smiling pleasure as she approached the table. She must have been successful because as the man got to his feet, his grin was a welcoming one. It softened the stern lines of his mouth and went some way towards allaying her fears about a stranger joining them. Especially when he held out his hand and said, 'I'm Marcus Glover. It's so very nice to meet you.'

His expression told her exactly how nice he considered it. In fact, his heavy-lidded eyes were gleaming with admiration as they roamed slowly over her, from the top of her head down to her feet. Her blush deepened. It had been so long since a man, any man, had displayed admiration for her that she'd quite forgotten how it felt. Or, more importantly, how to respond to it.

3

'It's nice to meet you, too.' To her relief, Petra felt her blush receding. She didn't want him to assume it meant she was attracted to him. She had no intention of becoming involved with a man.

'Come and sit by me,' Jenny invited. 'I'll tell you who's who in here. They're all locals.' And she proceeded to reel off a list of names which Petra had no hope of remembering.

'For goodness sake, Jen,' Debs remonstrated as she poured a large glass of wine for Petra, 'you'll blow the poor woman's mind. Here, get that down you. It'll help the old memory cells.' She grinned. 'Or not.'

'So, Debs,' Jenny put in, 'where's Ben tonight? Not at home, surely?'

'He is, yes. Babysitting. Otherwise I'm sure he'd have been out golfing or something.' Debs' tone was one of bitterness and sarcasm. Petra, startled by this unexpected change of mood, stared at her. 'You'll hear sooner or later, Petra, knowing how efficient the jungle drums are in this town, so I may as well be up front about it. Ben and I are having one or two problems. One of them the fact that he's suddenly turned into this mad keen golfer.' She snorted. 'At least, that's what he says he's doing on his numerous afternoons and evenings out. Me, I've got my doubts about that. Especially as another member of the golf club, who's also a friend of Ben's, mentioned he hadn't seen him in a while and asked how he was doing.' She shrugged. 'Anyway, I told him he can be the one to stay in this evening and look after the children he seems to have forgotten he fathered. We can't keep expecting my mother to step in and babysit. She already does it several times a week. And he needs to understand that I need some fun time, too.'

As if to emphasize this sentiment, she

took a huge mouthful of her wine, which promptly went down the wrong way, provoking a bout of frenzied coughing. When she looked back at Petra, her eyes were glistening with tears, and not just from the wine, Petra suspected. 'I — I don't . . .'

'Know what to say?' Debs bit out. 'I'm sorry. The last thing you need to hear about are my marital woes. So, tell me about yourself. You said you're here on your own?'

'That's right. My husband — well, he died not long after Christmas.' She paused, giving Debs the opportunity to say she was sorry.

'Actually, we'd been having some problems, too.' In a bid to steer the conversation away from herself, Petra went on to ask, 'Tell me about your children. How old are they?'

'Mollie's eight and Jack's six. They're the lights of my life. I adore them.'

Maybe that was the trouble, Petra reflected. Ben was neglected in favour of his children. It wouldn't be the first

60

marriage to have foundered for that reason. Not that she had firsthand experience.

'You don't have any children, then?' Debs went on to ask.

'No. My husband didn't want them, so . . .'

'Did you?'

'I would have liked a couple, yes, but as things turned out, maybe it's better I didn't.' Children had been something she'd desperately wanted. Grant hadn't, so that had been the end of that.

However, as time had gone on, her longing had intensified. It had been one of the reasons she'd begun her business. She'd needed something of her own; something to lavish her time and emotions on.

'Anyway,' Marcus cut in, 'I hear you're renting Sea View. I hope that means you're here to stay?'

'That's what I intend, yes. There's an option to buy it if I decide I eventually want that.'

'In which case, I hope you'll allow me

to take you out one evening. We could have dinner? Get to know each other a little better.'

Petra decided to put the kibosh on that straight away. 'I'm going to be busy — I hope. I'm planning to start up my business again.'

'You'll have your evenings free, won't you?'

'I don't think so, not at first. With the lighter evenings, I tend to work late.'

'So, what is your business? Maybe I can be of assistance? I have a lot of local contacts.'

'It's interior decoration.'

He made no attempt to hide his astonishment at that. 'You're a decorator?'

'Well, I like to think I'm a bit more than that,' she went on, trying not to take offence at his disparaging tone. 'I offer a variety of special effects and finishes. Something a bit out of the ordinary.' Now she sounded as if she was reciting from a brochure.

'I see. Well, good luck with that.' He

rolled his eyes at her. 'The residents of Poltreath aren't exactly known for their desire for design and innovation. Magnolia walls and white gloss paint are the norm.'

Once more, she decided it was time to shift the focus away from herself. 'Do you have a family?'

'I did. My wife and I divorced three years ago. I have one daughter, Sophie, eleven years old. She lives in Truro with my wife and her boyfriend. Well, her toy boy would be a more apt description. He's five years younger than her.' He didn't try to hide his contempt. 'At the ripe old age of forty-two, I'm dull and past it, apparently.'

'Oh, I-I'm sorry.' What did one say to a statement like that, other than to ask, 'Do you see much of Sophie?'

'I have her every other weekend and for most of her school holidays.'

'That must be a comfort for you.'

'Well . . . ' He pulled a face. 'Not always. I'm sure you recall being that age. Difficult is a mild description. She knows everything and I know nothing, apparently.'

'Ah.'

'Exactly.'

'So what do you do?'

'I'm in IT. My company provides individually designed websites for companies tailored to meet their needs. It's proving extremely profitable.' And he gave a smug smile, at the same time raising a questioning eyebrow at Petra.

She stiffened. Did he think that fact would make her change her mind about going out with him? If he did, he couldn't be further off the mark. She'd had her fill of wealthy men. The more success Grant had enjoyed, the more arrogant and critical of everyone and everything he'd become. Finn Hogarth's expression had reminded her of him when she'd had her brief encounter with him in town. If almost walking into his car could be described as an encounter.

'I'm also a fairly accomplished artist. Debs was telling me you might be joining our little band.'

He clearly didn't suffer from any sort of modesty. 'Yes. Painting is something I've often thought of trying.'

'Not that different to the day job, eh? Or maybe it is?' He cocked his head. 'In which case, do you think you're up to the challenge?'

She'd clearly upset him with her refusal to go out with him. But did he really think such a — well, ungracious response to her desire to join the group was going to make her change her mind?

'I'd have thought you'd have enough of painting with that as your main occupation.'

Petra didn't bother replying to that. Her first impression of him had clearly been way off the mark. He wasn't nice at all. In fact, there was something almost repellent about him. She wished he'd go. What sort of man thrust his way into what was intended to be a girls' night out?

Debs must have sensed Petra's dislike

65

of Marcus because she broke in, leaning closer to Petra and murmuring, 'I've spoken to Elizabeth Hogarth and she's very keen for you to go to the house and have a look at the rooms that she wants redecorated. She's open to ideas and she'd like a quotation if you come up with something a bit different. So I've said you'll ring her. If you take my advice, you'll go and see her. It'll be a really good job, almost the whole of the ground floor by the sound of it. She lives in a large house just out of town. Greystones.'

Marcus, looking thoroughly fed up by this time, got to his feet. 'I'll leave you to your business and your girl talk and get off. Things to do. Nice to have met you, Petra. You must seriously consider joining the art group. You'll be very welcome.'

And with that, he was gone. Petra couldn't help but feel relief, and some of that must have shown on her face, because Jenny said, 'I know, a tad smarmy.'

'Don't be cruel,' Debs admonished her. 'He's okay, really. I think he's lonely, and that Sophie's a real piece of work. Every time she visits him her hand's out for something, usually money. I wouldn't mind betting her mother puts her up to it. It would make anyone bitter.'

'Mmm. Well, I wouldn't touch him with a very long pole. There's something in the way he looks at you. Almost reptilian. I can't help but imagine a forked tongue shooting out — ' Jenny gave an exaggerated shudder. ' — and injecting a load of venom into me.'

★   ★   ★

The following morning, Petra mustered her courage and rang Elizabeth Hogarth's number. Elizabeth herself answered the phone and Petra launched straight into her fully prepared speech.

'I believe you're looking for someone to decorate.' She didn't get any further.

'You must be Petra.' Elizabeth spoke

in a lilting tone, almost musical, in fact. But it was the friendliness that she detected that really warmed her. It inspired an instantaneous feeling of affinity with the older woman. 'Deborah gave me one of your business cards. I'm very interested in what you do. I believe you offer something a little different?'

'I like to think so.'

'Splendid. Now, let me consult my diary. How would this afternoon suit you? Shall we say four o'clock? I have to be somewhere before that but I should be back by then.'

'That would be perfect,' Petra agreed, and after writing down the post code she turned off her phone. After which, she headed straight to the bureau where she'd stored her album containing photographs of previous work. From what Debs had said, this could be a very lucrative commission. Exactly what she needed to get her started.

Her confidence blossomed. She'd made two good friends. The sheer fun she'd had the evening before once the hateful Marcus had left them made that more than evident. The three of them were unmistakably on the same wavelength. She decided there and then to join the art group. She needed to immerse herself in local activities, and that way, maybe she'd succeed in putting the past behind her.

But when the moment arrived to get into her car and drive to Greystones, her misgivings returned. In spades. Supposing she couldn't pull this off? Couldn't live up to the Hogarths' expectations? She'd never had a commission as extensive as this one sounded. It wasn't just one room, as most of her previous jobs had been; it could turn out to be several if Debs was to be believed, and the fact was she'd always worked alone. Would Elizabeth be expecting a team of people? In her initial enthusiasm, was she aiming too high? She swallowed nervously as she put the postcode into her sat nav. But she'd agreed to go, so go she must. If the work looked too difficult, and she thought she couldn't handle it, then she'd turn it down. Simple. God, now she sounded like a bloody meerkat.

She turned the car out of her driveway, and following the sat nav instructions, took the next left which ran for a mile or so between the high hedgerows that were such a feature of Cornwall, then the next right for a few hundred metres before turning left once more onto the main road out of the town. She'd found a short cut, thereby missing Poltreath altogether.

She drove a short distance along this road before the robotic voice directed her to take the next left turn, and within a couple of minutes was informing her she had arrived at her destination. With her misgivings intensifying, she cautiously negotiated her way between the imposingly grand wrought-iron gates that confronted her — they must be at least ten feet high — and began to follow what looked like an endless driveway. She couldn't even see the house and could only presume it lay somewhere ahead. Acres of manicured lawn stretched out on either side of her, broken only by massive beds of herbaceous plants and flowers. Groups of trees, clearly chosen for their colours and architectural shapes, punctuated the rest of the garden. It resembled something that Capability Brown might have designed. She glimpsed someone working in one of the flower beds — the gardener, presumably. And then, as she swung round a sharp bend, she found herself confronted by what could only be described as a large manor house.

As the name suggested, it was built of grey stone, topped by a grey slate roof. Ornamental chimneys marched along the top of this. Dozens of stone mullioned windows ran in straight rows, two deep, along the front of the building, and there were even a couple of corner turrets.

Wow! It could have been Sleeping Beauty's resting place, except that there was no thorny undergrowth to hack a way through in order to reach her. Every instinct she possessed was screaming at her to turn round and drive home again. This looked way out of her league.

Nevertheless, she approached it slowly and came to a halt on a circular forecourt. A flight of shallow stone steps led up to the front door. She glanced around and to her horror recognised the Jaguar that had almost knocked her down. If she'd known Finn Hogarth lived here, she wouldn't have come within ten miles of the place. She could only pray that he wouldn't recognise her. He'd only had a fleeting glance, at best. There was also a BMW and a sporty-looking Mercedes, so she parked on the far side of the Mercedes, well away from the Jag.

With legs that shook, she climbed the steps to the front door. Even that was impressive, made of what looked like solid oak. It towered above her just as the gates had. These people evidently liked everything to be big. To intimidate callers? If that was the case, she'd put money on it having been Finn's idea.

For a second time she was tempted to make a run for it, but instead, she put out a hand and rang the doorbell. Should she have looked for a tradesman's entrance? If so, there was the first blot on her copybook. Before she had time to decide what to do, the door was pulled open and, to her horror, Finn Hogarth himself stood there, looking down at her.

Once again, she was struck by his good looks. Add to those the fact that he must be at least six feet two or three, and powerfully built, and she knew there was no way she would contemplate tangling with him. Given her height of a mere five feet four, she wouldn't have a hope in hell of emerging unscathed, or even alive.

'Um,' she stammered, 'I-I'm — '

'Petra Matthews,' he finished for her. So not only did he look alarmingly intimidating, but he seemed to be uncannily prescient as well. Although a moment's reflection reassured her that his mother had probably told him she was coming.

'Please come in.' He stood courteously to one side to allow her to do so.

'Th-thank you.' She didn't dare look up at him for fear of him recognising her. She needn't have bothered. His next words told her he knew exactly who she was.

'Glad to see you're in one piece.'

She did glance up at him then. Was he going to give her a dressing-down for stepping out practically into the side of his car? He looked the sort of man who'd do just that.

He didn't disappoint.

'Do you always step into a busy road without looking to see what's passing?'

'Do you always drive so fast in such a narrow road?'

He raised an eyebrow at her. He clearly didn't like his question being responded to by one equally critical.

Well, tough. She wasn't going to be cowed by him. Just because he was handsome and — and wealthy. And — big. And really, what sort of man would still be living with his parents at the age of thirty-eight? Defiantly, she returned his stare, hoping it would goad him into some sort of an apology.

Sadly, it had no effect at all, because he smoothly went on, 'Let's hope you're paying more attention today, then. My mother doesn't like not being listened to.'

Stung by his remarks, she pulled herself up to her full height, which meant her head only just reached the top of his chest, at the same time trying very hard to disregard the amused quiver of his mouth as he looked down at her. 'Of course I'll listen to her. That's what I'm here for. It's my job to give people what they want.'

His next words were throaty and barely discernible, but hear them she did. 'Is it, now? How intriguing.' He then glanced at her weighty bag before going on in the sort of tone that made her decide she must have imagined his provocative innuendo. 'I must say you look as if you've brought everything bar the kitchen sink with you, so let's hope you have something in there that will secure my mother's interest, otherwise you'll have had a wasted journey. And that would be a great shame.'

Again, it was a low murmur, and something flickered in his eye, something that looked remarkably like warmth. Maybe because of the gold glints that had appeared, which transformed the silvery-grey to amber, offering the perfect foil to his malt-whisky-coloured hair. It did give her reason, however, to think that maybe she hadn't imagined his initial innuendo. And it did seem to reinforce his reputation as a ladies' man. 'Give me your bag. It looks heavy.'

'I'm fine.' She clutched it to her chest. 'I'm perfectly capable of carrying a bag. It contains all my photographs and samples of work that I've done over the past couple of years.'

'Ri-ight. Well, in that case, please come this way.'

He led Petra into the biggest kitchen she'd ever been in. 'Mother, Ms Matthews is here.'

'Petra — please.'

'As you wish.' His eyes gleamed with what couldn't be mistaken for anything other than amusement. 'Mother, Petra Please is here.'

Petra stiffened with outrage as an elegantly dressed woman swivelled and regarded him with irritation. 'Finn, for heaven's sake, behave yourself. I apologise, Petra. He's quite harmless, really.'

'Good grief,' he scoffed, 'you make me sound like a dog.'

Petra stared at him. She didn't believe for second that he was harmless. For a start, he was dangerously handsome with his chiselled features and slightly aquiline nose. His perfectly formed mouth had widened in a smile which, she grudgingly acknowledged, only enhanced his looks. A fact she was quite sure he was only too aware of.

Pointedly ignoring him and his protest, Petra held out a hand to Elizabeth. 'Mrs Hogarth, I'm so pleased to meet you.'

'Call me Elizabeth, dear. If you're going to be working here for a while, I can't be doing with all that Mrs Hogarth business. Now, would you like some tea?'

'Okay. So, I'll be going now, Mother,' Finn put in. 'I have an appointment I can't miss.'

'Do you?' Elizabeth sounded surprised. 'At this time of the afternoon? Why don't you join Petra and me and have some tea? You'll be able to see what she has to offer.'

'Oh, I can see that already, and very nice it is too,' he added in the sort of provocative undertone Petra guessed was once again intended for her ears alone.

His glance slid over her, making her regret having dressed in a pair of figure-hugging jeans and a T-shirt that lovingly traced her breasts. She'd regained some of her lost weight, which meant her clothes fitted her again. She wondered whether all the men here were going to be so bold. Marcus had been the same, although Finn's glance didn't produce the deep aversion in her that Marcus's had. Finn's quickened her pulse and made her stomach clench with — what? It couldn't be desire, surely? Given his dubious reputation, he was the last man she'd be getting involved with.

Once he'd gone, she turned back to Elizabeth, only to find her grinning broadly. 'Ignore Finn, my dear. He's nowhere near as bad as he likes to pretend.'

'Really?'

'Yes, really. He enjoys teasing people, but it's always done kindly.'

Petra wouldn't have described his treatment of her as kindly. Far from it.

'He was always a naughty boy. He's not much better now. It's being an only child that does it.' Despite her words, her smile was a lovingly indulgent one. Elizabeth clearly adored her son. 'He needs a good woman ... ' She eyed Petra, eyes sparkling. ' ... to take him in hand.'

Petra stared at her, aghast. She couldn't have meant what that sounded and looked like, could she? As if she was speculating on Petra's suitability for that very role. Hurriedly, she pulled her album out of her bag. 'Right. Shall we have a look at this?'

'Let's have our tea first before getting down to business. We have plenty of time, don't we?'

So the two of them sat at the breakfast bar, talking as if they'd been friends for years. Eventually, when Petra spotted that it was after five thirty, she decided it was time to get down to the reason for her being here. She opened her album and spread it out before Elizabeth, her heart in her mouth, as she finally conceded that she desperately wanted this job, Finn or no Finn.

4

And, to her delight, it quickly became evident she was going to get it. Within moments of Petra opening the first few pages of the album, Elizabeth was crying, 'These look wonderful, Petra. That one especially.' And she pointed to the photo of a room where the walls had the look of ancient parchment due to the process known as frottage. 'That would be perfect in the dining room, with its oak wainscoting.' She then pointed to another. A finish created by colour washing. Not as time-consuming as frottage, but still a fairly slow process. 'This would be wonderful in the drawing room. So natural-looking. And I love the marbling effect. We must use that somewhere.'

'How many rooms were you thinking of having decorated?'

'The drawing room, the snug, the

dining room, the hallway and up the stairs, possibly the breakfast room, and the library needs updating a little, but as the walls in there are mainly covered in books . . . '

Good God. She could be employed for weeks, if not months. Which meant that somehow she'd have to avoid coming face to face with the maddeningly arrogant Finn — a difficult if not well nigh impossible task in the event that he did indeed live here. 'I have to tell you, it is just me, so . . . '

'My dear, that's fine. If it takes longer, that's okay. I'd rather have it done well than rushed. Oh — ' She regarded Petra anxiously. ' — do you have other jobs to do as well?'

'No. You'll be the first.'

'Excellent. Now, let's go and have a look at the rooms in question and you can tell me what you think.'

The tour took over an hour, with Petra offering her suggestions for each room, taking into account the preferences Elizabeth had already voiced.

Once Elizabeth had left her, she took photos of the rooms from various angles, as well as noting down all the measurements she'd need to work out the costings. The only things that troubled her were the walls in the hallway, in particular, the high one that stretched up one side of the stairs. She'd have to investigate the possibility of hiring some sort of platform and possibly scaffolding.

She gnawed at her lower lip. Was she being too ambitious? She'd never before embarked on a job so complicated or extensive.

Once she'd got all the information she needed, she returned to the kitchen to find Elizabeth. 'I'll work out the costs and get back to you with a final quotation as soon as I can.'

'There's no rush, dear. Take your time.'

As Petra drove home, her brain was reeling as the doubts about being able to actually do the job tightened their grip on her. It was going to take her hours and hours just to work out the cost of it all, never mind the task of actually carrying out the work. She was looking at several weeks, she estimated. Months, even.

By the time she got back to the cottage, she'd all but decided to turn the work down, but something, call it stubbornness, as well as pride in her skills, instructed her to stop being so pathetic. Okay, the job had its problems, but it would undoubtedly be profitable if she succeeded. But apart from that, it would also make an essential contribution towards the reputation that she needed to make a go of things. Somehow she'd cope. She had to. She needed the income.

From then on, she spent most of each day and part of the evening in front of her laptop until finally she arrived at the final figure. It was a huge sum of money. She couldn't charge that much, could she? But unless she did, it wouldn't be worth doing. She made a decision. She'd take her time considering all aspects of it, because once she'd agreed to do it, she couldn't then cancel. That would be unthinkable.

To stop her mind from endlessly listing each and every one of the difficulties she might encounter, and then struggling to come up with the solutions, she decided to attend that evening's art class. Thus, six thirty found her climbing the stairs to the upstairs room at the gallery. She walked in to be greeted warmly by firstly, Debs, then Isobel.

'You came,' were Debs' first words.

Isobel contented herself with a smug smile as she said, 'I thought you would. Meet Tara, my granddaughter.'

Petra smiled at the girl with Isobel. They were both sitting at easels. 'Hi, I'm Petra.' She offered a hand in greeting but was completely ignored. Tara simply stared at her for a moment before turning her head away, her lack of interest only too plain.

'Tara,' Isobel chastised, 'don't be

rude. Say hello.'

'Hello,' the girl said without bothering to glance at Petra. Petra hid a smile. Typical teenager. She was just amazed the girl had condescended to accompany her grandmother out in the evening. Most fifteen-year-olds would have point-blank refused such a thing. So there must be some kindness within her somewhere.

'Now — ' This was Debs speaking again. ' — have you managed to buy any paints, or anything at all? I would assume not, as you're not carrying anything.' She raised both eyebrows in amusement.

'No, sorry. I meant to come in and get some. I've been so busy.' She stared meaningfully at Debs at the same time mouthing, 'I've been working on a quotation for the Hogarths.'

Debs beamed her satisfaction at her. 'I'll go and fetch you what you'll need, then. Oils are the easiest medium to learn with. You can settle up next time you come in.' And she sped away.

Isobel laughed. 'Thank God for Debs. She has everything in that back room.'

'What are we going to be painting?'

'That.' She pointed to an arrangement of flowers in a glass vase with a couple of books to one side. It looked impossibly difficult to Petra. Especially the reflections in the glass vase.

'Petra.' She turned to see Marcus striding towards her. 'How are you? It's so good to see you here. Took my advice, eh?'

She didn't remember him giving her any advice. 'Well, I thought I'd give it a go.'

Debs reappeared, her arms full of the items that Petra would need to make a start. 'Okay. I've brought you a selection of brushes, oil paints, a palette board, turps, linseed oil, charcoal, pencils, and a canvas and easel.'

'Wow. Am I really going to need all of that?' Petra regarded it all doubtfully. How was she going to transport that lot back to the cottage? She'd walked in, not wanting the bother of trying to park the car somewhere.

'Did you walk here?' Marcus asked, evidently reading her expression of horror.

Petra nodded.

'No problem,' he said. His mouth tilted in what looked like immense satisfaction. 'I can give you a lift back.'

As loath as she was to accept his offer, she conceded she didn't have any other option. 'Thank you, that's very kind.'

'Okay, let's get started, shall we?' Debs cried. 'Everyone's here.'

Petra watched as they all sat down in front of their easels. She regarded her own doubtfully. It was folded up into what looked like a few wooden sticks bunched together and secured with a leather strap.

'I'll give you a hand if you like.' This was Marcus again.

'I've never done this before. It looks like some kind of Chinese puzzle.'

He laughed and swiftly erected the

easel for her. 'There you go.'

'Thank you — again.' She sat on the stool that Debs had just pushed behind her.

'Now, arrange your paints on the palette,' Debs had told her, 'just a small squirt of each, and then I'll help you get started.'

Debs turned out to be an excellent teacher, and before too long, Petra had the bare outlines of the subjects sketched out on the canvas. By the time the class was over, she was laying down the paint and could already see the rudiments of what the final image would be. She just wished Marcus would stop interfering. He was constantly moving to her side, issuing suggestions. Somehow she managed to hide her irritation. He was going to drive her home, after all. From now on, she'd bring her own car. There was a small car park not too far away. She was sure she'd manage to carry her things that far, or maybe Debs would let her leave them at the gallery.

'We're off to the pub now,' Debs called across as Petra was packing her things away into the bag that Debs had lent her.

'Well, Marcus is giving me a lift home, so I'm not — '

Marcus instantly interrupted to say, 'That's okay. We'll put our things in the car and walk back to the pub. I usually have a drink. I need one, in fact, after an evening's painting with Debs breathing down my neck.' And he laughed loudly, for all the world as if he'd cracked a joke, instead of all but insulting Debs.

And that was what happened. They congregated in the Ship once again. It was obviously the pub that the locals hung out in. It was also the nearest to the gallery. Eight of them packed themselves in around the largest table in the room. Isobel had had to go home because of Tara being with her; the girl was eager to watch a particular television programme. But Petra had seen the expression of longing on

Isabel's face as the others talked about enjoying a drink, and she wondered why she didn't drive the girl home and then return and join them all. She assumed they'd come by car, as they'd carried their painting things out with them. Still, that was a decision for Isabel to make.

As for Tara, she'd remained silently sullen for the entire time they'd spent painting. Petra wondered if she was always like that or if it had just been that evening.

They were on their second bottle of wine — well, Petra, Debs and a couple of other women were, while the men were drinking beer — and were growing increasingly raucous when who should walk in but Finn, accompanied by a startlingly attractive woman.

He noticed the group straight away, not surprisingly considering the din they were making. As his gaze homed in on her, his eyebrow shot up and his mouth tightened, before he said something to his companion and strode across to Petra's table.

'Petra,' he said. 'I wasn't expecting to see you here.'

'Weren't you? Why not?'

'I didn't have you down as a pub girl.'

'Pub girl?' she scoffed. 'What's that, then?'

His gaze hardened as did his jawline. 'Won't you introduce me to your friends?' He clearly had no intention of answering her question.

With a glance that was as cool as his, she indicated the circle around her and said, swiftly enough that he wouldn't have a hope of remembering the names, her small gesture of revenge for his remark about her not being a pub girl, 'Debs, Marcus, Elaine, Andrea, Jack, Dennis, and finally Ralph. Oh, and me-Petra.'

A flicker of gold lit the depths of his grey eyes as he spoke to the group at large. 'Nice to meet you all. Well, have a good evening.' He returned his gaze to Petra. 'How are you getting home? It's a good walk back to Sea View.'

Marcus chipped in at that. 'I'm taking her, old man. No need to concern yourself. She'll be quite safe with me.'

But, astonishingly, Finn didn't look altogether happy about that. Which was a bit rich given his own reputation with women. 'Well, let's hope so.' He swept his gaze back to Petra. 'Will I be seeing you at Greystones soon? My mother's keenly anticipating your quotation.'

Was he daring to question the length of time she had taken over it? She wouldn't be surprised. And how did he know where she lived? Elizabeth must have told him. Had he asked her? Almost certainly. Someone like him wouldn't want to be kept out of the loop. As a consequence of her irritated speculations, her tone was a waspish one as she told him, 'It's a big job, so I wanted to make sure I had it absolutely right. I didn't want to be accused of overcharging. She'll have it in a day or two.'

'Right. In that case, I'll be seeing you.' And he strode back to his attractive companion.

'Not if I see you first,' she muttered under her breath.

'Is there a problem?' Marcus asked. He'd clearly heard her remark, the last thing she'd intended.

'No. I'm not going to be working for him, I'm working for his parents.'

'Are you going to be decorating for them, then?'

'Hopefully, if Mrs Hogarth accepts my quotation.'

'Well, there's a turn-up.'

Petra was about to remonstrate with him over what sounded suspiciously like a sneer when Debs cut in. 'Was I right? It's a big job?'

'It's a massive job. I just hope I can do it justice.'

'I'm sure you will.' She slanted a glance at Petra. 'So, I assume you met Finn as well?'

'Yes. He opened the front door to me.'

94

'What do you think of him then?'

'I don't think of him,' Petra said, only too aware that Marcus was listening to their every word. 'He wasn't there for long.'

'Hmm.' Debs's gaze glittered with amused speculation. 'He seemed quite interested in you.'

Petra felt, rather than saw, Marcus's start of surprise.

'You want to watch yourself with him.' He sounded bitter; resentful, even. She fleetingly wondered if his wife and Finn had had something going at some time. Knowing Finn Hogarth as she was beginning to, and taking into account his reputation, as well as the good looks of his female companion, she wouldn't be surprised.

'Why's that?'

'He likes the ladies a little too much.'

'I've heard, so I shall be giving him a very wide berth.'

Debs laughed. 'Good luck with that then. The way I've heard it — what Finn Hogarth wants, Finn Hogarth gets.'

95

'Not this time, I can assure you,' Petra smartly replied.

She ignored the look of gratification that flashed across Marcus's face.

Eventually the publican called time and they all left, Petra and Marcus returning to where his car was parked. It was dark by this time and the street was empty of people. Petra admitted to feeling relieved that she wasn't alone. It felt sort of . . . creepy. This feeling was heightened by the sounds of their footsteps echoing off the buildings on either side of the narrow street. The earlier good weather had been banished by a heavy drizzle, the droplets of moisture beading her hair, as well as the shoulders of her jacket.

'This is very kind of you,' she told Marcus.

'Not at all.'

'It must be out of your way, though.'

'Well, a bit, but it's fine. Can't have you struggling alone — not in this weather.'

It wasn't until they reached the

cottage that she began to experience a sense of unease. She didn't know why. Marcus had behaved impeccably. He stopped the car and turned off the engine. 'I'll give you a hand with your things.'

'Thank you.'

They climbed from the vehicle and Petra carried the bag that contained the smaller items, while Marcus brought the easel and her partly worked canvas. She'd have to find herself a bag by next Thursday, as this one belonged to Debs. She struggled but did finally manage to open the front door. Marcus was standing close behind her. Too close. She could feel his breath on her neck 'Where do you want these?'

'On the floor will do.'

He put the canvas and easel down and straightened up.

Yet again, Petra said, 'Thank you so much.' She carried everything into the kitchen and set it all down on the table.

'It was no trouble.' Marcus had followed her in and was now looking at her, his expression one of expectation.

Her smile was barely there as she held out a hand to him. 'Well, goodnight and thanks. See you next week?'

He tilted his head, not taking the proffered hand. Instead, he regarded her from beneath lowered eyelids. 'Doesn't my good deed deserve a coffee, at least?' His mouth curved into a lazy smile, a gesture he evidently considered sexy. It wasn't. Mainly because his lips glistened with moisture, making her shudder at the notion of kissing him.

And even though she'd half expected something of this nature, she hadn't prepared a response. All she could think to say was, 'I'm tired, Marcus. I've had a very hectic week one way and another. Do you mind if we call it a night now?'

His smile vanished in an instant, as his eyes narrowed to slits. His voice when he finally spoke was heavy with — what? Displeasure? Hurt? No. It was more like indignation. 'Fine. I can take a hint. I'll see you round, then.' And he swivelled to stride, stiff-backed, into the hallway and towards the still open door.

She followed him. 'You certainly will. It's only a small town, after all.'

He swung to face her again, his gaze boring into her. 'It is, isn't it? Everyone knows everything here. So, be warned.' And with those curt words, he was gone.

Petra gazed after him. Be warned? What the hell did that mean? That he knew she was hiding something?

5

The following morning, Petra printed out her quotation for Elizabeth and then decided to walk into the town and post it. She should have asked for an email address. She needed to get her act together, and quickly, if she wanted to make the right impression on prospective clients.

It didn't take her long to reach the main street. She went directly to the post box halfway along before deciding to call in at the gallery to see Debs. She owed her for the painting materials, so that had to be taken care of.

'Hello, you,' Debs greeted her. 'Lovely morning. Glad that awful drizzle is gone.' She studied Petra for a moment. 'So, how did it go with Marcus last night?'

'Fine. Why?'

'Well, he can be a bit full on at times,

or so I've been told.'

'Full on?'

'Yeah, you know. So keen for a relationship, he's made a bit of a pest of himself once or twice.' She slanted a glance at Petra. 'I could tell he'd taken a shine to you.'

'Oh. He was okay.' Petra decided to leave it there. She was beginning to learn that gossip was rife in Poltreath, and she didn't want any criticism that she might make of him getting back to Marcus. She'd displeased him sufficiently with her refusal to offer him coffee. She didn't want to do anything to exacerbate that. She had more than an inkling that he might make an unpleasant enemy.

She paid Debs what she owed her and then said, 'I really enjoyed the class. How did I do?'

'I think you've got the makings of a good artist. Your eye for the shape of things and the variation in colours, as well as light and shade, is excellent. We'll soon have you painting murals for people. That would really be something different.'

'Yeah, in your dreams,' Petra scoffed, even though she'd had the very same thought herself.

'If you stick with it, you never know.' Debs regarded her seriously then. 'How did you get on with Elizabeth, by the way? Obviously you couldn't say much last night.'

'Great. I like her. I've just posted the quotation to her, so fingers crossed. It'll be a fantastic commission if I get it. Difficult in parts, but . . . ' She grimaced wryly.

'Well, if you need a bit of help at times, I know a very good chap. He's reliable, and he's always looking for extra work. Maybe you could use him for the basic work, leaving you to concentrate on the more difficult stuff?'

'We-ell, I've been a little nervous about the stairway. The one wall is higher than anything I've ever tackled before.'

'I've got his card somewhere.' Debs

walked towards a desk in the corner of the gallery. 'The high wall right at the back of the gallery is his work. Also the upstairs rooms.'

Petra walked across the room to take a look. It was a high wall, not as high as the one at Greystones, but high enough. It was well painted, the finish evenly executed. 'That's good.'

'Got it.' And she waved a card at Petra.

Petra took it and read, Rob Pascoe. Reliable decorator. Reasonable rates. 'Thanks. I'll keep this.'

'Do you fancy a coffee while you're here?' Debs regarded her, her expression a hopeful one.

'Do you mind if I don't? I thought I'd take a walk while I'm out. If I'm going to be working, I might not get many more chances.'

If Debs was disappointed with this response, she gave no indication of it. 'Okay. See you next Thursday? If not before?'

'You certainly will.'

* * *

Petra decided to return to the cottage first and drop off her purchases. She'd thought she might venture up to the headland. So far, she'd given it a wide berth, being nervous of heights. But living in Cornwall as she now did, with its rugged and steep coastline, it was a phobia she needed to overcome.

With the decision made, and once she'd offloaded the shopping, she braced herself and set off up the steep and stony pathway. But despite the difficulty she experienced negotiating it, it didn't take long to reach the cliff top, and the views when she did were spectacular. Strangely, the height didn't bother her, but even so, she stood a foot or so from the edge.

The day was a sunny one, so she began to walk, maintaining her distance from the cliff edge. She hadn't gone far when she spotted Isobel walking towards her.

'Hello,' she hailed the older woman.

'Gorgeous morning, isn't it?'

'Glorious. I couldn't resist the idea of getting a breath of fresh air, as well as a bit of time to myself.' Isobel gave a deep sigh. 'It's lovely having the family staying but it can get a bit — well, you know, intense.'

'Is everything okay?'

'Yeah. But Tara can be difficult. Teenage tantrums. Sally's a bit too indulgent at times.' She gave a rueful grin before briskly saying, 'But I'm sure you don't want to hear about my troubles.'

'I don't mind if it helps you to get it off your chest.' She paused, unsure whether to go on or not. 'I noticed she was very quiet last evening, for a girl her age.'

'Yes. She's had a hard time these past few years. Sally's . . . ' She paused. 'Well, she gets depressed, which doesn't help. And there is only the two of them, most of the time, that is.' Again she paused. 'I'm sure you've heard about my husband, Tom, and the pension fiasco.'

'I have, yes. I'm so sorry. Have you had any news of him?'

'No, nothing. I don't let myself dwell on it too much or I'd go out of my mind with worry. I have to trust that he'll return home sooner or later. If only he'd realise, we'll manage somehow.' Her mouth tightened. 'If that wretched man, somebody Cornell, hadn't killed himself, I'd do it for him.'

Petra took a deep breath. Everyone hated Grant.

It was immediately evident that Isobel had noticed her reaction to her angry comments. 'I'm sorry. I shouldn't go on. It's my problem, no one else's.'

In an attempt to distract Isobel from her own response to the angry words, Petra said, 'Is there anything I can help you with, if that's not too presumptuous of me?'

'No, not at all. But the truth is, there's nothing anyone can do. Other than offer me a job. You'd think with the summer season almost on us, the hotels and cafés would be looking for people. I think they must all want somebody younger.'

'Could your daughter not help out? Maybe she'd have more luck.'

'She's tried. But it's got round that she's not really reliable.'

'How long have the two of them been with you?'

'Five weeks, give or take. After Tom disappeared.'

'It must be very hard for all of you.'

'At times, yes. Tom was always so good with Tara. Despite not seeing her all that often — she and Sally lived just outside of Plymouth — he seemed to know instinctively how to deal with her, and — and she listened to him. She misses him dreadfully. But I'm sure there are people far worse off than me.' She smiled shakily. 'So, how are you settling down here?'

Glad of the change of subject, because she couldn't help her feeling of guilt over Isobel's troubles — all down to Grant and his fraudulent dealings

— Petra readily answered. 'Fine. I love the town and everyone's so friendly.'

'What made you come here?'

'I fancied a change of scene after my husband died.'

'Yes, I was sorry to hear about that. How did he die?'

It was the sort of question Petra dreaded. 'H-He'd been ill for a while.' Which wasn't actually a lie. He had looked ill for a while, and no wonder, since he was being investigated for fraud.

Isobel looked at her, her expression one of sympathy. 'No family to help you cope with things?'

'Not really, no. In the end, I decided it was time for a new beginning.'

'Well, good luck. Anyway, I'd better get on. Lots to do at home. Oh, here's someone else having a walk.'

Petra glanced around and saw a medium-sized chocolate-brown and white dog. There wasn't anyone with him.

'Whose can he be?' Isobel asked. 'I don't recognise him, or her.'

'I've never seen him before,' Petra

said. She had a quick look at the animal. 'It's a she. She must have run off from somewhere, or someone. Here, girl, here.' She crouched down and held her hand out to the animal. She came to her, slightly gingerly, but she did take a sniff at her fingers. Then it was as if she decided that Petra could be trusted and came closer, rubbing against her legs.

'Well,' Isobel laughed, really laughed for the first time, 'she's obviously taken to you.'

Petra searched for a collar and name tag, but she wore neither.

'That's strange. Do you think she could have been abandoned?'

'It's a possibility, I suppose. If not, I'm sure her owner will be looking for her. I'll ask around as I go back. She's probably got a microchip implanted. Don't owners have to do that these days?'

'Haven't a clue, but if you'd ask around, that would be great. I'll do the same. Someone must be missing her.'

★   ★   ★

Petra walked on, the dog tracking her every step. When she sat down on a bench, the animal patiently squatted at her side, and when she stood up again to carry on, the dog followed suit.

Petra looked down at her. 'Who do you belong to, I wonder?'

The dog barked softly in response, at the same time wagging her tail enthusiastically. When Petra returned to the cottage, the dog accompanied her. Petra was at a loss as to what to do. She couldn't simply take the animal in. She must belong to someone. Hardening her heart against the mute appeal in the brown eyes, she closed the front door behind her. But the pitiful look on the dog's face almost broke her. And when she started crying, Petra succumbed and opened the door.

'Come on then, but I must find out who you belong to — if I can.'

She rang Debs at the gallery and described the animal to her.

'I don't recognise the description. Perhaps you could take her to an animal sanctuary? There's one on the way to Bodmin, I believe.'

Petra then rang Jenny. But Jenny didn't recognise the description either. 'Debs mentioned an animal sanctuary near Bodmin?'

'Yeah, I heard it's closed down. Lack of funds.'

So that was that.

She found a bowl and filled it with the contents of a tin of tuna. The dog hungrily devoured it, licking the bowl so clean it positively shone.

She then rang both of her friends again and told them she was taking the dog in temporarily. 'But could you put a card in your window, asking the owner to contact me?'

Petra stood looking down at the dog. 'What's your name, hmm? Who do you belong to?'

★ ★ ★

By Sunday evening, and when no one had appeared at her door asking for their pet, she began to allow her growing affection for the animal to take hold. Even so, she decided to take her to a local vet and see if they could read her chip, supposing she'd had one implanted. It would supply the owner's name and address, she presumed.

She hadn't been chipped, however. The vet told her, 'It should have been done. All owners are required by law to do so. Sadly, an awful lot of people don't bother.' He looked at Petra. 'What will you do with her?'

'I'll keep her for now and see if someone does come forward. I've put cards in a couple of shop windows in the town.' But the truth was she'd be heartbroken if someone did turn up on her doorstep. 'If no one appears soon, though, I'll bring her here and have her chipped myself.'

'I'm going to call you Kelly,' she told the animal on the way back to Poltreath; the vet's practice had been a couple of miles out of the town. 'After a very dear friend of mine who emigrated to Canada.'

She then drove to the pet shop she'd passed on the way to the vet's and bought dog food, two bowls, a lead and a collar, and lastly, a bed. She also bought a couple of toys, a rubber bone and a rubber ball, hoping she wasn't wasting her money.

For the first time since her world had collapsed around her, Petra felt content; happy, even. Kelly was a joy. They began to go on long walks, ensuring that Petra met many more local people. They would stop and chat to her, at the same time, making a fuss of Kelly. There was no sign of recognition, and Petra began to feel she belonged here. Hopefully her troubled past was becoming just that; her past.

And when Elizabeth Hogarth phoned her and told her she had the job of decorating the entire ground floor of the house, that was truly the icing on the cake.

She picked Kelly up and waltzed

around the kitchen with her, lavishing kisses on the ecstatic animal. 'I've done it. I'm going to have a decent income again. A business of my own.'

Elizabeth had suggested she pay a twenty-five-percent deposit up front and another twenty-five percent halfway through the job. The final fifty percent would paid be on completion.

Which was a huge relief, because Petra had been worrying about how she would fund the work on her limited budget. Now she could start buying what she needed. She'd brought some of the smaller items with her in the back of the car, such as her brushes, et cetera, but she hadn't been able to fit in the larger items, like a stepladder and her trestle table. She'd have to buy those. Luckily, her car had fold-down seats in the back, so she'd be able to transport smaller items. But she would look out for a very cheap and hopefully not too old van.

She paid a second visit to Elizabeth to clear up some of the finer details and this time met her husband, David, who proved to be every bit as likeable as his wife. He confirmed Elizabeth's initial assurance that they wanted the very best and if that took longer, then so be it.

'Now,' Elizabeth said, clapping her hands together, 'let's have some tea.'

Petra decided there and then that working for this charming couple would be like working for family. They were so warm and friendly. In fact, they were instantly on first-name terms, insisting she call them by their Christian names, which she already did with Elizabeth, though she hadn't expected such easy warmth from David. He reminded her of Finn. The same chiselled features, the same pale grey eyes. But it was within Elizabeth's expression and smile that every now and again she caught a flash of Finn.

They sat in the kitchen, like last time, to drink their tea, and Elizabeth began to probe for details of Petra's life in Worcestershire. For the first time then,

Petra began to feel edgy; uncomfortable. She hated deceiving people, especially people like these. However, she kept to her fabrication of Grant having been ill and subsequently dying.

'You know,' Elizabeth suddenly said, 'I feel as if I know you. Have you visited Poltreath before this?'

'A couple of times, yes,' Petra quickly said, deciding to stick with the story she'd already told Jenny, 'with my husband. He loved Cornwall.'

'Maybe that's it, then. Are your parents still alive?'

Petra nodded.

'What do they do?' Elizabeth was determined to find out all about her.

Petra felt her heart sink. 'My father's general manager of an engineering business in Chester. My mother took early retirement from teaching.'

'They must miss you. Are they going to be visiting? I'd love to meet them. You could bring them here.'

'Elizabeth,' Davis gently chided. 'For heaven's sake, stop. The poor girl's beginning to look beleaguered under all these questions.'

'Oh, dear me.' Elizabeth, crestfallen, instantly apologised. 'I'm so sorry. I didn't mean to pry. I simply can't help myself.' She gave a slightly self-conscious laugh.

'That's all right.' Petra mustered up a smile. 'My mother's the same. Loves to know what makes people tick.'

'So, you must have lived in Chester too, then?' Elizabeth blithely disregarded her husband's sigh of resignation.

'Originally, but I've been living in the Midlands since I married. A very small village. You wouldn't have heard of it.'

'I might have. Try me.'

'Compton Green,' Petra reluctantly said. Elizabeth wouldn't have heard of it, surely?

'Do you know, I have heard of it.' Elizabeth frowned. 'Now, how would I have done that?'

Petra gnawed at her bottom lip. How stupid of her. No, more than stupid, utterly insane. Whatever had possessed her to tell them that? She'd allowed their warmth and friendliness to beguile her into a dangerous indiscretion, one she couldn't now take back. Supposing Elizabeth remembered where she'd heard the name? She was a smart woman. She'd soon put two and two together.

Petra's insides twisted with dread.

'Has it been in the papers for some reason? Compton Green. I'm sure I know it. David?' Elizabeth glanced at her husband, but he just shook his head.

Speech was beyond Petra. What the hell had she done?

Even as she had that thought, the sound of the front door opening reached them. Elizabeth leapt from her stool.

'That must be Finn. He said he might call in when he knew Petra would be coming.' She raised a saucy eyebrow and rolled her eyes at Petra. 'I do believe you've made a conquest, my dear.' And she actually winked then.

'He doesn't normally visit when we discuss household matters with someone.'

Petra too climbed off her stool. As if things weren't bad enough in the wake of her utter stupidity, Finn Hogarth was about to put in an appearance. Could he have recognised her, too, and come to alert his parents to the fact that they were about to hire the wife of a fraudster to decorate their home? She wouldn't put it past him to have made a few enquiries.

She awaited his appearance, her heartbeat so tumultuous she could barely draw breath. Supposing Elizabeth told him what Petra had just said? Would that jog some memories for him as well? Could her new life be over before it had really begun?

6

Resisting the temptation to take to her heels and run, Petra waited for Finn to walk into the kitchen. Once he had, she'd make her excuses and leave, all the while praying that Elizabeth wouldn't mention either her suspicion that she'd seen Petra somewhere before or the name of the village that Petra had come from.

However, before she had chance to say anything at all, Finn had walked in and was demanding, 'Is that your dog out there?'

'Um — yes, it is.'

'Well, he's going crazy in the back of your car. He's — '

'He's a she.' Petra's tone was a curt one. 'Kelly; her name is Kelly.'

He tilted his head sideways and regarded her with what looked like irritation. Clearly he didn't appreciate

120

being interrupted. 'She has probably ripped your upholstery to shreds by this time.'

Petra tightened her lips and snapped, 'I doubt that.' She'd taken care to park her car beneath a large tree on the edge of the drive so that it was well into the shade and had left all the windows partly open. It wasn't a hot day, so Kelly should have been fine, otherwise she'd never have left her there.

'I didn't know you had a dog,' Elizabeth put in, obviously keen to tamp down what seemed to be developing into an argument. 'Why didn't you bring her in?'

'She's a stray. She followed me home a few days ago and as no one has claimed her, I decided to give her a home. But I won't bring her in. Thank you, though, for asking. I really must go.'

'Oh, but you can't. Finn has only just arrived.'

Finn continued to regard her, but rather than with irritation now, his mouth had curved into a smile and his eyes were gleaming with something that couldn't be mistaken for anything other than amusement. The gold glints that she'd spotted a couple of times before had appeared, warming the coolness of the grey that they normally were.

'I think Petra has decided that's a very good reason for her to leave.'

An eyebrow lifted, bestowing an almost demonic look upon him. She lifted her gaze, fully expecting to spot a pair of horns sprouting through his hair. Of course, there weren't any.

Petra didn't know what else to say then other than to weakly protest, 'Oh, no, that's not why —'

'Good.' Elizabeth beamed at them both. 'I'll make another pot of tea then. You go and fetch — Kelly? from your car. We can't leave her out there. You can show Finn what you're going to be doing for us. I know he wants a couple of rooms redone in his house, don't you, Finn?'

'I certainly do,' he murmured. 'And I

122

can't imagine anything more pleasurable than having Petra there — doing it for me.'

This time the innuendo was unmistakable. His expression told her exactly what he meant. He was attracted to her, and had every intention of doing something about it. Still, she now knew he didn't live here, so she wouldn't be at risk of bumping into him on a daily basis.

Fortunately, all this passed Elizabeth and David by. Elizabeth was busily making a fresh pot of tea, and David had picked up a newspaper, so Petra had no alternative but to fetch Kelly. Just as Finn had told her, Kelly was leaping around, barking loudly. She must be bored, Petra decided, because the interior of the car was still in the shade, so she couldn't be too hot. The second she saw Petra, her tail began to wave from side to side, and she cried with relief. Petra was filled with remorse. How thoughtless of her. Kelly had feared she'd been abandoned again.

'Come on,' Petra said. 'We've been invited for tea, so you be on your very best behaviour. I don't want any shenanigans.'

As Kelly leapt from the back of the car, Petra swivelled to find Finn standing in the doorway watching her.

'No, no shenanigans, Kelly.' And he gave a shout of laughter.

Stung by the manner in which he was once again mocking her, Petra glared at him as she clipped Kelly's lead on. He really was the most annoying man. The dog, to her relief, walked obediently alongside her as she entered the house.

She went into the kitchen, hoping and praying that her hostess would have forgotten all about her somewhat dim recollection of both Petra and the name Compton Green.

'Oh, she's gorgeous.' Elizabeth crouched down by the side of Kelly and began to stroke her. Kelly immediately lay down and rolled onto her back, exposing her stomach for further rubbing. 'I've always wanted a dog, but David's allergic to fur — oh dear.' She widened her eyes at her grinning husband.

'It's okay. I've got some phone calls to make so I'll leave you all to it. It's been very nice to meet you, Petra.'

'It's nice to meet you, too, Mr — um, David.'

Elizabeth got up from Kelly's side and began pouring the tea. 'Would Kelly like something? Some water?'

'That would be kind,' Petra said. 'And then we really must be going.' She began to gulp her tea, despite the fact that she was in danger of scalding her mouth. 'I need to take Kelly for a walk and then I'm going to an art class. I need to get home and get my things together.'

'Oh, how interesting,' Elizabeth said. 'Where do you go for that?'

'A room above the art gallery — in Fore Street.'

'Oh, I know it. I also know Debs who owns it, but, of course, you know that. It was Debs who put me on to you in the first place. Or was it the other way round? You on to me? Anyway, it doesn't matter. So what are you painting?'

'A still life. It was my first attempt last week.'

She became aware of Finn listening intently to all of this. 'Have you not painted before — well, other than walls, obviously?'

'No, but it's something I've always wanted to do.'

'I bought a couple of paintings from her a few weeks ago,' Elizabeth said. 'You'll have to let me see yours when you've finished.'

'Oh,' Petra laughed, 'I don't think it'll be worth paying good money for.' As she had finished her tea by this time, she got to her feet.

'When do you think you'll be able to make a start here?' Elizabeth fortunately seemed to have forgotten her wish for Petra to show Finn what she'd be doing in the house. 'And I must give you the deposit we mentioned.' She reached for the handbag that was sitting on the worktop and pulled out a chequebook. 'I'm afraid I'm still old-fashioned enough to write cheques. Is that okay with you? I don't quite trust all this online banking. You hear such dreadful stories of hackers defrauding people out of all of their money.'

'It's fine,' Petra told her. Then, keen to get away from the sensitive topic of financial fraud, in case something about the words jogged Elizabeth's memory as to where she'd heard — or worse, read — the name Compton Green, she swiftly went on, 'I have to get hold of the materials that I'll need to begin, so shall we say a week on Monday?'

'Perfect. Where will you be starting?'

'The dining room, if that's okay?'

'It is. I'm so looking forward to seeing what you can do.'

'Me too,' Finn drawled, as yet again an amused glint illuminated his eye.

Petra ignored him.

'I'll see you out,' he then said.

'There's no need,' Petra muttered.

'I insist.'

Sensing that there was no point in further argument, Petra headed out of the kitchen and into the hallway, Kelly at her heels. They were all outside before Finn spoke again.

'I'd like to invite you out one evening for a meal.'

Petra stood stock still at that, and stared at him, making no attempt to hide her astonishment.

'Why so surprised?'

'Well, I-I hardly know you.'

'Well, you can get to know me over dinner.' Heavy lids now shuttered his expression. 'Just as I'd like to get to know you.'

'And what would your girlfriend think about you taking me out?'

'Girlfriend? What girlfriend?'

'The one you were in the pub with the other evening.'

'Oh, that was Emily. Her husband's a good friend of mine. Well, so is she.'

'I'm sure she is.' Petra's sarcasm was unmissable, just as she'd intended it to be.

Finn's jaw hardened. 'Jake, her husband, knows we go out when he's away. We've all been friends since schooldays. And for your information, that position is vacant at the moment.'

'What position?'

'That of my girlfriend. Would you be interested in filling it, do you think?'

'No, I wouldn't. And nor do I want to go out for a meal with you. I'm going to be rather busy — in your parents' house for the foreseeable future.'

'You'll have your evenings free, won't you?'

'We-ell, yes, but I have no intention of getting involved with anyone.'

'I'm only inviting you for dinner, not asking you to marry me,' he drawled. 'I'm quite harmless, really.'

Who did he think he was fooling? He looked about as harmless as a ravenous wolf preparing to rip a lamb apart.

'No, I'm sorry. I'm far too busy at the moment.'

'You must have some free time, surely?' His tone was an exasperated one, which just went to prove her theory. He didn't like his wishes being thwarted.

'No. I often work late, especially if I'm halfway through a particular task. Sometimes I simply can't leave it, and with the lighter evenings . . . ' She shrugged. 'I have to make the most of what time I have.'

'You'll need to get back to walk Kelly though, won't you? Or do you intend that she walks herself?'

Her only response to that was to glare at him. But all he did was to bat away her glare with a grin, indicating beyond any shadow of doubt that he knew he'd got the better her. Of course she would have to get back for Kelly. But she wasn't about to admit defeat. There was no way she was going out with a notorious womaniser like Finn Hogarth. Mainly because she had a strong suspicion that he would be more than capable of inflicting unbearable pain upon her if she should weaken and succumb to his self-assured arguments.

7

Sadly, her escape didn't go as smoothly as she'd hoped because Finn tapped on her window. Grudgingly, she opened it, albeit, a meagre couple of inches.

'If you should change your mind about dinner, here's my card.' And somehow he managed to thrust it through the miniscule gap, giving her no choice but to take it. 'Just give me a ring.'

A fleeting glance showed her his phone numbers, mobile and landline, his email address and house address: Poltreath Manor. Judging by the name, he too had a large house, along with the substantial wealth that Jenny had already mentioned. 'As I've already told you, I'm going to be busy, so don't hold out any hopes.'

'How about I just hold out my hand?' And, with yet another feat of ingenuity, he succeeded in getting his fingers through the couple of inches that were all that was available to him.

Defeated by his sheer determination, she sighed and lowered the window.

His mouth quirked at the corners. 'You can shake it. You won't be committing yourself to anything.'

He really was insufferable. However, she did shake his hand, albeit briefly.

'Goodbye,' she muttered, beginning to rev the accelerator in her impatience to be gone.

However, he wasn't done yet. 'I'll ring you,' he said.

She took her foot off the accelerator. 'What?' She ground the single word out between clenched teeth.

'I'll ring you to fix a date.'

Her eyes widened. Fix a date — with him? No way. Hadn't she made herself clear enough?

' — for you to come and see what I want done. To my house,' he smoothly elaborated, his expression telling her he was all too well aware of what she'd been thinking. 'A couple of rooms need redecoration.'

'Oh — I see. Well, it won't be for a while.'

'Don't you have any help?'

'I usually work alone. I prefer it that way.'

'Okay, but if you need someone, I know a couple of good guys who are always on the lookout for work.' He pulled back slightly, glancing over her car. 'And you'll need something more suitable than this, surely, for transporting your materials and equipment? You won't get a decent-sized step ladder in, for instance.'

'I'm going to be looking for a van. A cheap second-hand one.'

'I might be able to help there. I know of one that's for sale, for a very reasonable price. I could take you to see it.'

There really was no stopping him, was there? He was like a steamroller, flattening every argument she put before him. Nevertheless, could she afford to turn this offer down? She couldn't.

'Well, if you give me the name and address of the person who's — '

'It's better I take you. He won't try and bump up the price if I'm there. He knows me. I've dealt with him before.'

She eyed him doubtfully. Was this a ploy to get her to agree to go out with him?

'It's up to you, of course.' His tone was a casual one, but still, she didn't trust him. 'If you want, ring me tomorrow when you've had a chance to think about it, and we'll fix something up.'

'Thanks,' she muttered.

'Okay, then. I'll be seeing you.'

Petra pressed hard on the accelerator and the car leapt forward. She couldn't believe it. He was going to have his own way, after all. Because if he helped her find a van, she could hardly then refuse to have a meal with him, could she?

★ ★ ★

Despite all Petra's efforts to banish Finn Hogarth from her thoughts, she found it impossible to do so. Even during her walk with Kelly, his face, his eyes, lingered in the forefront of her mind. It was obvious he expected her to yield to his request to take her out, especially in the wake of any assistance he might give her in the purchase of a van. But could she afford to turn down his offer? She couldn't pay too much, yet whatever vehicle she ended up with, it was essential it was reliable as well as economic to run. And as she knew little or nothing about the workings of a car, or rather, van engine, it really was a no-brainer.

Eventually, it was time to leave Kelly asleep in her bed and drive to the art gallery. By the time she got there it was six thirty-five, but the other painters were only just erecting their easels and laying out their paints. She opted for a spot next to Isabel and Tara, hoping that as well as distracting her from thoughts of Finn, Isobel's chatter would deter Marcus from joining her. But the moment he spotted her, he strode across and began to set up his own easel.

'You don't mind me joining you, do you?'

Resigned to the inevitable, Petra said, 'Not at all.' She glanced Isabel's way to see if she minded, but all she did was smile at Marcus.

She then turned to Petra. 'Have you managed to do any more painting at home?'

'I haven't. I suspect I'd find it difficult without being able to see the subject.'

'Why don't you take a photograph? Mind you, Tara hasn't touched hers either, have you, darling?'

Tara ignored her grandmother, her brow pulled down into a scowl as she began to paint.

Isabel murmured, 'We're not in a very good mood.'

'I can hear you, Gran,' Tara snapped. 'Will you just leave me alone?'

Instead of reprimanding the girl, Isobel asked, 'So, what have you been doing, Petra?'

'Well, I decided to keep Kelly.'

'Kelly?'

'Yes, the dog that followed me home. No one has come forward to claim her, and she isn't chipped so . . . '

'Oh, I see. Well, she'll be company for you if nothing else. You are in a very lonely spot.' She carefully added a couple of brushstrokes to her canvas before asking, 'Where did you live before? Was it as isolated as Sea View?'

'Not really.'

Isobel turned her head towards Petra. 'So where were you?'

'Worcestershire A small village. You wouldn't have heard of it.' She wasn't going to make the same mistake she'd made with Elizabeth.

'Try me.'

'No point. Nobody's heard of it. It's not much more than a hamlet. I don't think it's even on a map.'

'Oh, well, of course, if you don't want

to tell me, that's your prerogative.' But Isobel was obviously miffed by Petra's reticence. So much so, that after raising her eyebrows at Marcus, she turned away from Petra and carried on painting in silence, the atmosphere between them increasingly glacial.

Petra wondered if it would be better to tell her. The chances were she'd never have heard of Compton Green. 'Isobel.'

But all Isabel did was sniff somewhat disparagingly and turn even further away, talking instead to the woman on her other side.

Petra couldn't believe what had happened. Even Marcus had begun giving her odd looks instead of speaking. Which actually was no loss, but it did mean that by the time the class was over, Petra had decided she wouldn't go for a drink; she'd go straight home.

She was busily packing her things into the large bag she'd bought especially for the purpose when Debs came across to her. 'Are you okay, Petra?' she quietly asked. 'Come over here.' And she jerked her head sideways, indicating they should move away from the others and any chance of being overheard. Petra went willingly.

'You're looking a bit down. Are you depressed about your painting?'

'No, not at all. It's just — I think I've upset Isobel.'

'Oh, I shouldn't worry too much about that. I don't want to sound harsh, but the truth is, it doesn't take much to upset Isobel, especially since she's had Sally and Tara living with her. I know she's finding life tough at the moment, but she really shouldn't make the mistake of driving her friends away.' She eyed Petra. 'What did you do? Or say?'

'I wouldn't answer some of her questions, that's all.'

'Too personal, were they?' Petra nodded. Debs lowered her voice to a whisper. 'A tiny warning — Isobel's got a very long nose. She likes to know everything about everyone; she always did, even before Tom vanished. The trouble is she then broadcasts it all over town. Of course, what she doesn't realise is that local people now simply label her as nosy and keep things strictly to themselves.'

All Petra could think was, thank goodness she hadn't told Isobel what she wanted to know. Even if she didn't recognise the name Compton Green, somebody else might.

So it was with a sense of relief that she left the gallery and drove home. However, that was relatively short-lived. Because a little later, while she was walking Kelly, she spotted Isobel approaching along the road. She decided to try and make amends for her reluctance to answer Isobel's probing questions. She didn't want to make enemies here; she wanted friends. Needed friends.

'Hello.' She greeted the other woman with a smile. 'You also in need of some fresh air?'

Isobel made no effort to respond, other than to snap, 'Yes.'

'No Tara, then?'

Isobel gave an exaggerated glance around. 'As you can see — no.'

Trying not to take offence at the sarcastic nature of the remark, Petra concentrated on admonishing Kelly. 'Stop that.' She frowned down at the animal who was enthusiastically sniffing Isobel's shoes. She took her time in glancing back at Isobel, only to find her staring, her eyes narrowed with speculation.

'I'm sure I've seen you somewhere before. I've been racking my brains trying to remember where.'

'I don't think you can have,' Petra said. 'Although I've been to Cornwall, it was a long while ago, and then we didn't stay here in Poltreath.'

'We? You mean your husband and you?'

'Yes, but it was a few years ago — '

'Maybe that's it. I've somehow remembered you from then — although it feels much more recent.' She gave Petra another searching look. It was as if she were trying to see right inside her.

Petra was practically squirming by this time. 'Maybe I've got a double somewhere; a doppelganger? Anyway, I'd better get on. Kelly's getting impatient.' Which was patently a lie, because Kelly had stopped her sniffing and was sitting patiently at Petra's side.

'Is she? She looks fine to me.' Isabel's gaze sharpened. 'So, tell me, how are you really liking it here? A bit different, I would imagine to — now where was it? Oh yes, of course, Worcestershire. I have friends in Worcestershire. They'd most likely know your — *hamlet*. They might even have known you — and your husband.'

'Sorry, I really must go,' Petra said for the second time. A growing sense of panic meant that the perspiration was peppering her brow. She could only pray that Isobel didn't notice. Judging by the expression on her face, it was more than evident that she already suspected that Petra wasn't being honest with her. Petra wasn't surprised. She'd never been good at lying. Her mother, for one, had always been able to see straight through her. Her teachers had had the same gift.

'I know.' Isobel's tone now was one of sarcasm. 'Kelly's getting impatient.' Once again she stared down at the dog, who instantly wagged her tail, showing no sign of wanting to go.

Petra couldn't believe the transformation that had taken place in someone who'd initially been so friendly. It was as if an unseen hand had flicked a switch. 'Well, it's been nice to see you,' she said, starting to move away.

'Likewise,' Isobel coolly responded. 'Will I see you next Thursday?'

'I-I'm not sure. I'm going to be pretty busy from now on.'

'Really? With what?

'I'm going to be working at the Hogarths'.

'Decorating, presumably? I spotted your cards in the gallery.'

'Yes, that's right.'

'I presume you've had experience in that field of expertise?'

'Yes. I had my own business in Worcestershire.' Isabel's eyes narrowed at her. 'Well, you've really landed on your feet here, then.'

This time it wasn't just sarcasm that laced her tone, it was envy; malice, even.

'Well, I wouldn't have put it in quite those terms.'

'Wouldn't you? All I can say is — for a newcomer, you've very quickly established yourself in the right circle. I've lived here for most of my life and never got as much as a hello from Queen Elizabeth.' And she strode away without saying anything more.

Petra stood staring after her. Queen Elizabeth? Where had that come from? Anyone less majestic and proud than Elizabeth she couldn't imagine. Still, she had an uneasy feeling that despite her efforts to get along with people, her unwillingness to answer Isobel's probing questions had made her an enemy.

That night, Petra got very little sleep. Instead she was tormented by the memories of bricks being hurled through her windows, of paint being plastered over doors, and people, strangers, standing outside chanting 'Thief, thief, you're not wanted here.' When she did finally fall asleep, she was plagued by disturbing dreams. She even awoke at one point convinced she'd heard glass breaking somewhere in the house.

Of course she hadn't, which she swiftly discovered when she crept downstairs, Kelly at her heels, to check. But altogether, she was deeply disturbed and full of the sort of dread she'd been forced to live with in Compton Green and which had ultimately driven her away.

* * *

Come Saturday morning, Petra had made her decision. As much as she was loath to ask Finn Hogarth for anything, she needed a van and he'd said he could help her get one. Before she could chicken out, she picked up her phone and rang him.

'Finn Hogarth speaking,' he answered.

'I-It's Petra Matthews . . .'

'Well, hi there. What can I do for you?'

It was a perfectly innocent question, but for all that, Petra thought she detected an undercurrent of sensuality. Her doubts resurrected themselves. What would she be getting herself into if she accepted any kind of favour from a man like him?

'Y-You mentioned knowing of a reasonably priced van.'

'So I did.'

The silence went on until it became embarrassing. 'So — um, I was wondering if I could go and see it?'

'You surely can. I'll come and collect you.'

'I can go alone.'

'I wouldn't hear of it. I know Jack,

who's selling it, and he can be a bit of a rogue at times. He'll give you a far better deal if I'm there as well.'

Hah! Another man who'd be perfectly prepared to take advantage of a lone woman. A surge of exasperation flooded through her. How did she know they hadn't planned this together? That Finn hadn't already told this Jack that he'd found a mug to buy his van? It would probably turn out to be an old rust bucket, years past its sell-by date.

'So,' Finn continued, 'it's nine thirty now. I'll be with you by ten thirty. Okay?'

'Oh — uh, yes.' She hadn't expected it to happen that speedily. 'Will he accept a cheque? Or does he only take credit cards? Or I could transfer the money online if he'd prefer that?' She was gabbling now, something she invariably did when nervous.

She could hear from his voice that he was grinning. 'We'll sort that out when we get there. If you decide to buy it, that is.'

Her mouth tightened. He thought she was an idiot. She'd certainly jabbered on like one.

'I'll see you in an hour then.' He was still grinning, she was sure of it.

* * *

By the time the hour had passed, her feeling of disquiet over what she was about to do had magnified ten times over. When ten forty-five arrived and there was no sign of Finn, her misgivings were replaced by anger. Did he think she had had nothing better to do than hang around waiting for him? With her anger intensifying by the second, she dialled his phone number only to hear the engaged tone. Perfect! He was busy chatting while she was forced to kick her heels. If she had any idea where it was they were going, she'd drive herself there, and blow Finn Hogarth. As it was, it was almost eleven o'clock before she detected the purr of his Jaguar as it pulled up outside.

She grabbed her jacket and went to the front door. She yanked it open and walked straight into him. She hadn't expected him to be right there on her doorstep. She took a hasty step back and as a result lost her balance. She felt herself begin to topple backwards. He reached for her, grabbing the tops of her arms and pulling her into him.

'I don't often get a welcome like this,' he murmured, his mouth a mere inch from hers. 'Can I assume you're pleased to see me?'

She shook his hands off her, too furious to even speak for a moment. 'Hardly. You're . . . ' She checked her wristwatch. ' . . . half an hour late.'

'Sorry. I was detained; unavoidably detained. A phone call. It was someone I really needed to speak to.'

'Whereas I wasn't. I could be left kicking my heels — '

He stared at her, his narrowed gaze wandering from her furious eyes, to her hotly flushed cheeks, and then down to her parted lips. Petra felt as if he were

149

physically touching her; caressing her, even. Her breathing quickened.

'I'm truly sorry.'

She didn't respond. Instead she swivelled, taking care no part of her touched him, and closed the door behind her, while simultaneously struggling to harden her heart against the plea in Kelly's eyes. They'd barely been parted since the time she'd taken her in.

'You're upset.'

'You've guessed.'

They reached the car and Finn opened the passenger door for her. Still, she couldn't resist saying, 'A phone call would have been nice, to explain your tardiness.'

'A bit hard to do as I was already on the phone.'

She glared up at him. That had come out a bit too smoothly and, what was even more maddening, he'd deftly wrong-footed her. In silence, she seated herself as he closed the door. While he strode to the driver's side, she glanced around the interior. It was immaculate, with cream leather upholstery and inlaid veneer panels, as well as every conceivable gadget and electronic aid to make for easy driving. It was the epitome of luxury and an unwelcome reminder of Grant and his profligate spending.

Finn climbed in and started the engine. He slanted a glance at her. 'Right. Jack's place is four or five miles from here. I've phoned and told him we're on our way.'

'Oh, you managed to phone him, then?' She knew she was being petty and churlish, but she couldn't seem to help herself. If she went on like this, he'd probably throw her out of the car; she wouldn't have to exit under her own steam, as she was sorely tempted to do.

'Look, I'm very sorry I kept you waiting. It was rude of me, but can we let it go now?' And he turned his head and gazed directly into her eyes.

She stared back, her heart racing as

151

her stomach lurched with — what? Desire? Did he know how handsome he was? How downright sexy? She suspected he did and wasn't above using that fact for his own ends.

'Yes, it was.'

He held a hand out to her. 'Am I forgiven?'

She took it. 'Yes.'

'Thank you.'

She eyed him with suspicion. He had sounded too meek to be true. And she didn't have Finn Hogarth down as a meek man, far from it. Arrogant was a much more apt description, as she'd already decided more than once. She belatedly realised then that she was still holding his hand, and what was more, his fingers were gently caressing hers.

She tugged them free. He pressed his foot on the accelerator and the car smoothly and silently moved forward.

Their destination, when they reached it, turned out to be a small, somewhat ramshackle garage incorporating a repair shop and a couple of fuel pumps on the forecourt. Four vehicles stood there. A medium-sized white van was one of them. She regarded the figure stuck to the windscreen with astonishment. For a vehicle of that year, 2017, it was remarkably cheap. Was there something wrong with it?

A portly middle-aged man strode towards them, grinning broadly. 'Finn,' he said, 'haven't seen you in a while.'

'No, I've been rather busy.'

'Hah! Making another million or so, no doubt.' Jack chuckled. 'So, who's this then?' He looked at Petra, his expression one of undisguised interest and speculation.

'This is Petra Matthews. I rang you? She's looking for a reasonably priced van, so as I'd seen your advert in the paper, I mentioned it to her.'

'Oh yeah, so you did. I'd forget my own head if it wasn't attached to my body.' He gave another chuckle. 'This would be just the ticket, even if I say so myself. Reasonable mileage — very, and even more reasonably priced.'

Petra decided it was time she said something. 'It seems too cheap. Is there something wrong with it?'

Jack immediately glanced at Finn. But all Finn did was shrug his shoulders.

Petra regarded them both. What was going on here? Some sort of deal between the two of them?

'There's absolutely nothing wrong with it.' Jack was looking distinctly affronted. 'I want a quick sale, that's all. You're welcome to give it a test drive.'

She glanced again at Finn. There was no indication of any sort of guilt on his good-looking features. In any case, why would he do a deal with Jack over a cheap van? And for somebody else? 'Okay.'

Jack held out the keys to her. 'There you are, then. You going with her, Finn?'

'Of course.'

Petra glared at him. Did he think she wasn't up to test-driving a vehicle? 'There's no need for that.'

'I think there is. I doubt you know this area. We wouldn't want you getting lost.'

Petra couldn't argue with that. Her sense of direction had never been good, although she wouldn't admit that to him. She had no trouble picturing the smug expression that would appear upon his face. Instead, she climbed into the van's driving seat and started up the engine. Finn climbed in alongside of her and waited in silence while she cautiously manoeuvred the van into the road. She'd never before driven any sort of commercial vehicle and she wanted no mishaps.

But as she turned left and headed for the roundabout that she could see at the top of the hill, she became aware of Finn's gaze resting on her with rather more frequency than was warranted in her opinion, and her nervousness intensified to an uncomfortable degree.

8

Despite the unease that Finn's scrutiny induced, it took only minutes for Petra to decide the van was exactly what she needed.

So when he asked, 'What do you think? Will it do?' she unhesitatingly replied, 'I think so. I can't hear anything wrong with it.' Hah! As if she'd know.

'Okay, good. So turn right just ahead. That will take us back in a circle to Jack's.'

Within minutes, she was pulling onto the garage forecourt where Jack was waiting.

'Everything okay?' were his first words.

'I think it'll do fine.'

The formalities were swiftly completed and she agreed to pick the van up in five days' time. It would then be hers, taxed and insured, and ready to drive away.

'I'll bring you to collect it,' Finn said.

'There's no need. I'm sure Debs will bring me, or I can come by taxi.'

'As you wish.'

His ready acquiescence took Petra by surprise. Could she really have got away with it that easily? No pressure to go out with him in return for the favour he'd done her? Maybe he hadn't been serious in the first place.

It wasn't until they were pulling to a halt in front of the cottage that he said, 'I'm hoping you'll join me for a meal this evening.'

Ah, that was more like it. Superb tactics on his part. Lull her into a false sense of — what? Confidence that she'd got away with it before moving in for the kill? Or was she being too judgemental?

She turned and looked at him. He looked straight back.

'I'd really like to spend some time with you, get to know you better.'

'Would you?' She couldn't hide her scepticism.

'Yes. I like you, Petra. Is that so wrong? So unbelievable?'

And put like that, she couldn't disagree. She shrugged her shoulders.

'What does that shrug mean?'

'Well, you must have several women only too eager to go out with you. You've only just met me.'

'Why should that make a difference? You intrigue me. There's something . . . mysterious about you. As if you have secrets, depths to explore.' He paused. Then: 'You're also very beautiful, enigmatic; inscrutable, even.'

Was she really? Was that what was attracting him? If only he knew what those secrets were. Would he still feel the same way then? She doubted it.

'Is there someone else? Is that it?'

'No.'

He cocked his head to one side and studied her intently. 'My mother told me that your husband died just a few months ago. I'm very sorry, but . . . '

He paused, as if working out the best way to say something. ' . . . the truth is, you're a young woman. You have to start living again. I'm sure your husband wouldn't want you to remain alone.'

'Are you?'

'Well, as sure as I can be.'

'So not sure at all, then.'

'What is it, Petra? Did you make a promise of some sort to him?'

She shook her head.

'There won't be any strings; it will just be a meal. I won't push you any further than you want to go.'

'Okay.'

'Okay?' He looked genuinely shocked.

'Yes, okay. I'll have a meal with you.'

He was right. She'd already embarked on a new life by the simple act of moving here. The natural progression from that was to start seeing other people; other men. And, let's face it, she owed no loyalty to Grant, considering the troubles he'd left behind him.

He gave a wry smile. 'Well, don't

159

sound too eager, will you? It might go to my head.'

'Sorry.'

He didn't say anything for a full minute; he simply scrutinised her from beneath lowered lids. Then: 'That's sorted, then. I'll pick you up at seven thirty. I've been invited to dinner at a friend's house and they suggested I bring someone.'

That had been the last thing she'd expected. 'Um, I don't know. I assumed you meant just the two of us.'

'Would you rather it was just you and I?' The corners of his mouth twitched in a half-smile. 'I thought you'd feel safer in company.'

'Safer? You just said you wouldn't push me any further than I wanted . . . ' Did he, after all, have something more in mind than just dinner?

'And I won't. I merely thought — being with other people . . . ' He was beginning to look bemused; baffled, even.

'It's fine. You're right. It will be more

. . . comfortable.'

'Comfortable?' he scoffed. 'I've never been described in quite that way before when taking a woman out. I don't know whether my pride is mortally wounded or merely dented.'

'Oh, I didn't mean — '

'So what did you mean?'

'Well, I-I suppose that it will make conversation a bit easier with several of us. That's all.'

He gave a shout of laughter then. 'Okay. I'll take your word for it. But I promise the next time we go out, it will definitely be only two of us.' His tone was now full of promise.

And there it was. The trap he'd set had sprung neatly but securely closed around her. How could she now say no to a meal with him — alone?

Stung by what she interpreted as his deliberate entrapment of her, her tone was a curt one. 'Will it be very formal? Only, I've not brought many clothes with me.'

'Oh, no. Casual, well — smart casual,

161

I suppose. But really, Jeannie's very easygoing, as is Rob, her husband. Anything will do.'

'Is that whose house we're going to?'

'Yes. We're all old friends.'

Nonetheless, panic began to make itself felt as she mentally reviewed her limited wardrobe. She belatedly regretted not having brought at least a couple of her designer outfits with her. Still, it was an excuse to buy something new. And there was a dress shop in the town, although she hadn't ventured inside yet.

'Don't look so worried. We don't stand on ceremony here.'

She opened the car door and climbed out. She could hear Kelly barking inside the cottage. She turned to face him again. 'Thank you for today. It was a great help. The only thing that's bothering me is the price of the van.'

'Too expensive?'

'God no, the exact opposite. Far too cheap, surely? I'm a bit worried there might be something wrong.'

'Look, take it from me, there's

nothing wrong with it. You had a good buy, so just be thankful. Jack was having a good day.'

She stared at him. There was a strange expression on his face, one of almost embarrassment. She recalled the look of collusion between the two men. As she'd wondered then, could Finn have made some sort of deal with Jack? In fact, could he have made up the difference in the price Jack asked and the real selling price?

'Um — you didn't . . . ?'

'Look, I must go. There's someone I have to meet. I'll see you later.'

Quickly she closed the car door, allowing him to perform a U- turn and leave before she could say another word. She'd expected him to insist on seeing her to her door. The fact that he hadn't only made her all the more certain she was right. He'd partly paid for the vehicle, and hadn't wished to be quizzed about it. But why would he do that? To help her out? But again — why? Could Elizabeth or even David

163

have had a hand in it? That seemed more likely.

She turned and went into the house. Kelly greeted her ecstatically.

'I know — you want a walk. Give me ten minutes and we'll go.'

* * *

Fifteen minutes later, they were heading into town and to the dress shop she'd noticed on her previous visits. Once there, she had a quick look in the window at the display before going inside. She closed the door behind her and instructed Kelly to sit down.

The saleswoman immediately came over to them and bent down to fondle Kelly's head. 'What a sweet dog.'

'Yes, she is,' Petra agreed.

'So,' the woman said, straightening up, 'how can I help you?'

'I want something suitable for dinner at a friend's house. Nothing too formal, but a bit smarter than day-to-day things.'

'Well, I have a couple of outfits that might meet your needs.' And she proceeded to pull a dress and a skirt with a matching top off the rack that ran along one wall of the shop.

They both looked gorgeous. The dress was a beautiful shade of jade. And the skirt and top were patterned in shades of burgundy, aqua and taupe.

'I'll try both,' Petra impetuously said.

'I'll take you into the fitting room, then.'

Once she'd slipped the dress on, she loved it. It hugged the shape of her body, tracing the perfectly proportioned curves, enhancing them in fact, and testifying to the fact that she'd regained the weight she'd lost. The neckline revealed her cleavage without being too obvious about it, and the skirt ended just above her knees. The two-piece was equally flattering, with its dipping neckline and snug bodice. The skirt was slightly longer than the dress and softly draped to swirl attractively around her legs. A wide burgundy leather belt completed the outfit.

'I love them both,' she told the saleswoman, 'but they're a bit too expensive. I'll have to choose one.' And she looked at them, quite unable to decide.

'I can do you a deal,' the woman said 'Both of them for . . . ' She named a figure that was utterly irresistible.

'Done,' Petra instantly told her. They were outfits she could wear almost anywhere, and when all was said and done, she could afford to treat herself for once. And if her business took off as she hoped it would, well, she'd be able to afford any number of outfits like these.

'I also have shoes, if you're interested? Those are on sale too, to make room for my new stock, which is due in any day now.'

All of which meant that Petra returned home well pleased with her day's purchases, although the matter of the van and its price was still niggling at her. She sighed. If Finn had paid part

166

of the asking price, she'd feel duty-bound to repay him. And that could mean that a hefty portion of the deposit Elizabeth had given her would be swallowed up.

But first of all, there was the question of which outfit she should wear. She held them both up and tried to decide between them. The dress was the more elegant, the two-piece less so. But Finn had said smart casual, so it had to be the skirt and top.

Once she had it on, she eyed her reflection in the mirror. The top was very fitted, even more so than the dress, as well as displaying the rounded tops of her breasts. She hadn't noticed that in the shop. Was it too much? Would Finn take her provocative display as an invitation, some sort of come-on?

In the end, she opted for the two-piece, deciding she was more than capable of dealing with any amorous advances Finn might be driven to make.

By seven twenty she was ready and so

on edge she decided to have a glass of wine, which she promptly swallowed in just a couple of mouthfuls. 'That's better,' she murmured. 'Bring it on, Finn Hogarth. Just try anything and see what you get in return.' Although quite what she meant by that, she had no idea.

And she was fine until she heard the sound of a car pulling up outside and, peering through the window, spotted Finn's Jaguar. Her breathing quickened as her pulse raced into hyperdrive. She was tempted for one second to hide — or better still, feign illness.

But when the doorbell chimed, she straightened her shoulders and firmly told herself, 'For goodness sake, you're a thirty-year-old woman, not a teenager. What can he do to you in someone else's house?' Nevertheless, she couldn't help asking herself, what about when they returned here? Would he expect to come inside?

With no answer to that question, she went to the door and opened it. She'd decided she didn't need a jacket, as it was such a mild evening, so she was forced to watch as Finn's smouldering glance swept over her, lingering on the low neckline for several seconds before moving on down over the rest of her, to finally return to her face, his expression unmistakably signalling that he liked what he was looking at; liked it a lot. Which ensured she immediately changed her mind. She grabbed a jacket from the back of the door and slipped it on.

'You look gorgeous. In fact, you surpass all my expectations.'

'Really? So what were you expecting? That I'd be wearing my work clothes, maybe?'

He grinned, setting her pulse racing once again. 'No, I just hadn't dared imagine it, in case the sight sent me completely insane.' The words were uttered so softly, so huskily, she had to strain to hear them, even though he'd moved closer to her. So close, in fact, she could feel his breath feathering the

169

skin of her face, and smell his aftershave.

But when she did hear what he was murmuring, she felt herself blushing hotly. She couldn't take him seriously, could she? To try and calm her own emotions as well as his, she directed what she hoped was a cool glance into the eyes that were still gleaming just a couple of inches away from her. 'Really?'

'Petra,' he murmured, still huskily, 'you are a very beautiful woman. You must expect men — me — to respond to that.'

'Shall we go?' Even she could detect the sound of desperation in her tone, so for sure Finn would. How the hell was she going to deal with him if things got even more heated between them? So much for her confidence in her ability to do just that.

'Certainly.' He offered her an arm, but she'd turned back to bid farewell to her pet, who was sitting, hopeful of a walk.

'I never thought I'd be ignored in favour of a dog. That's definitely a first,' he drily concluded.

Petra felt her blush deepening, and this time she took hold of the proffered arm and together they walked to the Jaguar. Once they were both seated and Finn had driven off, Petra asked, 'How far away do your friends live?'

'A five-minute drive. Pencarrow Bay. Do you know it?'

'I've heard of it. I haven't been there yet.'

'It's very scenic. They have a house overlooking the sea.'

'It sounds gorgeous.'

'It is. I almost bought a house there, but in the end I plumped for the one I'm in now. More privacy. The bay is a bit touristy, what with all the hotels. We're almost there.' He swung the car off the main highway and took a smaller side road. A golf course stretched away on the one side. On the other side were several hotels, some not much bigger than a large house, but two of them were very substantial. They passed a road that led down to the bay and a beach, judging by the signpost, and then, turning right, Finn pulled onto the driveway of a double-fronted red-brick house.

Several cars were already parked there: a BMW, a Porsche, a low-slung sports car — she wasn't sure what that was — and a large Mercedes.

'The others are all here,' Finn said.

'Others?'

'Yes. Four other friends have been invited too. All friends of mine.'

Petra hadn't reckoned on that. She'd expected it to be just her and Finn and their hosts. Her heartbeat increased as her pulse rioted. It was a reaction she'd had over the past months, each and every time she was forced to meet someone new. She invariably feared the signs of recognition in their eyes, the horrified cry of, 'You're the wife of that awful man, that fraudster.' She repeatedly told herself it was yesterday's news, and people forgot. But then someone, as had happened a couple of times recently, would say, 'Have we met before? I seem to know you,' and all the horror and guilt that she'd felt at the time would flood back.

'Are you all right?' Finn asked. 'You look very pale.'

She looked at him and saw the frown of concern upon his face.

'They're very nice people — honestly.'

'I-I'm fine,' she assured him.

When he continued to regard her doubtfully, she added, 'Really,' and even managed a small smile.

Once they were out of the car, he placed his hand on the small of her back and shepherded her up the shallow flight of steps that led to the front door. He then rang the bell while Petra fidgeted nervously by his side. He glanced sideways and said, 'Stop worrying.'

'I'm not.'

'Yes, you are.' His gaze slid over her tense features. 'Everything's going to be fine.'

But the minute the door flew open and a petite woman with a mane of auburn hair stood there smiling at them, Petra knew it wasn't. Their hostess was dressed in skinny-legged jeans and a low-cut T-shirt. Petra only just stopped herself from groaning her despair out loud. She was totally overdressed. She should have been warned by the fact that Finn was wearing a pale blue open-necked shirt and a pair of cream chino trousers. No jacket. But she hadn't taken any notice. She'd been far too aware of the way he'd been looking at her. Hungrily — as if he was imagining her in his arms. She glared accusingly at him. He must have known it would be casual; very casual, in fact, as opposed to smart casual. But all he did was raise an eyebrow and say, 'Petra, meet Jeannie. Jeannie, meet Petra.'

'Hello, Petra. Finn has told us about you.' And she smiled saucily as she held out a hand for Petra's jacket.

Petra again glared at him. What the hell had he been saying?

'All good, trust me,' Jeannie went on with a throaty chuckle. 'Finn, stop glowering at me.'

She then reached out for Petra, dragging her in to land a kiss on her cheek. 'Welcome, Petra. Now, come in and meet the others. We don't stand on ceremony here. We've all been friends for years. Love the outfit, by the way. Where did you get it?'

And with those simple yet obviously sincere words, Petra felt herself relax. 'From Greta's, in Poltreath.'

'You did?' Jeannie looked surprised. 'I'll have to go and have a look. The place obviously has hidden depths.'

Petra followed the tiny woman — she couldn't be much more than five feet one or two, and slim with it — with Finn right behind her to enter a large sitting room in which five other people all stood, drinks in their hands, mutely regarding her. They too were dressed very casually, although one of the women did have a skirt and blouse on, thus alleviating some of Petra's discomfort.

175

'Let me introduce you.' Jeannie took hold of Petra's arm and led her into the centre of the room. 'First, my husband, Rob.'

A tall grinning man held out a hand to her. 'Hi. Good to meet you, Petra.'

Jeannie then indicated one of the other two women, the one in the skirt. 'This is Judith.'

Petra took the outstretched hand and murmured, 'Nice to meet you.'

The woman, a good bit taller than Petra, unabashedly looked her up and down, a glint of something — Petra wasn't sure what — in her eye, as she said, 'So you're Finn's latest fling, are you?'

Petra sensed Finn stiffening at her side as she realised the glint in Judith's eye was scorn.

'Um — well, no, I wouldn't . . . '

'Petra is a friend, Judith, and a very clever designer,' Finn instantly chided.

Judith's eyes narrowed. 'Designer of what?'

'Interior design. I do a range of

special paint effects.'

'Oh.' Judith gave a snort. 'You're a decorator. How quaint.'

'No, not simply a decorator. As I said, I offer a large range of specialised finishes. Marbling, frottaging . . . ' She stopped talking abruptly. She was beginning to sound like a sales brochure again.

'She's going to be redoing my parents' house, Judith,' Finn filled the sudden silence, 'and you know how particular my mother can be.'

If that was intended to be some sort of reassurance, Petra agonised, it hadn't worked. It simply piled yet more pressure upon her. The truth was, she was feeling more and more out of her depth. She was dressed wrongly — Finn's fault, she deemed — and now, to add insult to injury, she'd become the object of this woman's derision.

Jeannie cut in at this point. 'And this is Duncan, Judith's husband.'

Petra found herself looking at another tall well-built man. To her relief, like her host, his face wore a warm smile. It was a stark contrast to his wife's hostile demeanour. Such was Petra's relief at this that her smile was a radiant one, illuminating her eyes and bestowing an attractive flush to her cheeks. 'I'm so pleased to meet you, Duncan.' Again, she disregarded Judith's low snort.

'As I am to meet you. You dog, Finn. Where did you find this gorgeous woman?' He chuckled, sublimely oblivious to his wife's glare of disapproval. As for Petra, she couldn't stop her own laugh.

To her surprise, though, Finn didn't respond to these remarks. Instead he remained silent, and when she glanced sideways at him, it was to see his features set rigid and almost as disapproving as Judith's. His gaze when it met hers was as cold as ice, steely in fact, which made her wonder if he was resentful, or even jealous, of the warm manner in which she'd responded to Duncan's admiration. After all, she had never, not once, responded to him with such warmth. She ventured a smile at him by way of apology, but sadly it landed on stony ground.

She turned her attention back to Jeannie, who was saying, 'And these two are my oldest friends.' She looked totally unconcerned by the sudden tension in the air. 'Dominic and Rosie. We went to school together.'

Petra smiled at Rosie and received a broad grin in return. 'Lovely to meet you, Petra. That's a very unusual name.'

'Yes. I blame my mother. I was conceived — or so she maintained — right after she and my father visited the city of that name while on holiday in Jordan. I'd much rather have been called something like Rosie. Or Judith.'

But her attempt to ease the tension that was lingering in the room proved futile. What was worse, much worse, was the manner in which Judith was staring at her, gimlet-eyed and with a dawning yet puzzled recognition. Petra felt her stomach clench. She knew, with total conviction, what was coming next.

She wasn't disappointed.

'Have we met before?' Judith asked, her eyes so narrow now they were no more than slits.

She might as well have left her hair blonde and her eyes blue, Petra miserably decided, because her attempt to change her appearance had failed dismally. And if one more person asked her that particular question, she feared she'd scream out loud. However, on this occasion, she managed to restrain herself and simply said, 'I don't think so. I'm sure I'd have remembered.' She prayed that only she heard the tremor of her voice.

'Strange. I could have sworn . . . '

'For goodness sake, Judith,' Duncan broke in, 'you're always thinking you know people and you're almost always wrong. Give it a rest. You read too many newspapers and magazines.'

Petra's breath froze in her throat at that last remark. Would that be all it took to jog Judith's memory?

But all Judith said was, 'I'm sure I

know you. It'll come to me. It usually does if I just give it time.'

It was then that Dominic laughed and said, 'I'm quite sure if it had been me who'd seen Petra before this, I'd have no trouble remembering exactly where and when.' He winked at her.

Petra didn't dare look at Finn, but even so, she sensed his irritation, if not anger, at the reactions of the two men to her. It was this wretched top. Why the hell had she worn it? It was way too revealing; it invited men's comments and attention — women's too. The last things she wanted.

'Dominic,' Rosie said, feigning annoyance. 'He's harmless, really, Petra.' She grinned broadly.

Dominic instantly slid his arm around his wife and pulled her close. 'The truth is, she's the only woman for me and she knows it.' He dropped a kiss on her cheek.

But in spite of Dominic's good-natured comments Petra remained agonisingly aware of Judith's lingering suspicion, while all the time wondering whether she was ever going to be free of her past and her husband's crime.

9

Even though Judith's narrowed gaze returned to her again and again, and her own dread of her identity being somehow disclosed intensified, Petra found herself actually enjoying the evening. The food was delicious, and everyone — apart from Judith, that was — went out of their way to make her feel welcome. Even Finn seemed to have put his jealousy — if that was what it had been — to one side. Although why on earth he should be jealous over her, she couldn't imagine.

Nonetheless, as he was sitting almost opposite her, she couldn't help but be aware of his glance resting upon her more and more frequently as the evening progressed. Once in a while, emboldened by the wine she'd drunk, she returned his stare from beneath lowered eyelids, then watched as his

183

eyes darkened and his breathing noticeably quickened. And throughout it all, she couldn't stop thinking about their drive home — through the darkness — though it would only take a few minutes. Her heartbeat raced as she wondered how she would react if he tried to kiss her. She had an uneasy feeling she'd let him. For the truth was, and against her will entirely, she was finding herself increasingly drawn to him.

So when, at twelve thirty, he looked across at her and said, 'Shall we go?' her emotions and senses began to zigzag all over the place, mainly, she suspected, because she'd had far more to drink than she should have. It had been Judith's doing. Her gaze had remained a keenly searching one, making no secret of her stubborn resolve to recall where she'd seen Petra before. Which meant that Petra's only respite from her sense of dread had been to allow her wine glass to be filled more times than she knew was sensible.

'If you're ready — then yes,' she softly murmured.

'Oh, I'm ready,' he equally as softly replied, his smouldering gaze burning into her.

It was her turn for a quickening of her breathing, causing her breasts to rise and fall; a display that Finn made the most of. In fact, he looked like a man well and truly aroused by his passions. What had she done? What she'd done, she admitted, was to meet and then hold his gaze, flirtatiously and wantonly, and with increasing frequency. And now he was undoubtedly expecting her to fulfil the promise she'd seemed to be making. She swallowed hard and tried to get to her feet, only to promptly drop back down onto her seat again — hard.

She saw him struggling to hide a grin as he got up and strode round the table to her. And that was a large part of her problem. The fact that they'd remained sitting at the table, nibbling at cheese and grapes, and constantly refilling

185

their wine glasses. He reached her, and placing both hands around her waist, lifted her to her feet.

She gave a giggle and protested, 'I'm fine and perfectly capable of — of . . .'

'I know you are,' he gently agreed. 'I'm simply trying to be a gentleman.'

'Hah!' Judith scoffed. 'You — a gentleman? That'll be the day.'

Finn ignored her, guiding Petra from her chair towards the door and the hallway.

'I'll get your jacket, Petra,' Jeannie hurriedly said.

Oh, good Lord. They could all see that she'd drunk too much. Whatever must they be thinking? She met Duncan's eyes and he winked at her. Dominic contented himself with a wicked grin. Then they all got to their feet.

'It's been so good to meet you, Petra,' Rosie said. 'We must all get together sometime, at our house.'

'Oh, well, I might be a bit busy from now on.'

'She'd love to, Rosie,' Finn cut in.

Petra glowered at him. The cheek of the man. How did he know what she wanted to do? His only response, however, was a maddeningly complacent grin.

'Come along,' he said, helping her with her jacket. 'I think we'd better get you home.'

Well and truly stung now by his patronising words, she wrenched herself out of his grasp, only to find herself immediately staggering sideways. His arm shot out and he grabbed her, tucking her into his side, this time keeping his arm firmly around her.

Jeannie laughed and kissed Petra. 'It's been a real pleasure, and I mean that. Perhaps we could meet for a coffee sometime,' she whispered, 'just you and I.'

'I'd like that,' Petra whispered back. 'You can tell me all about Finn.'

'Oh, boy. Have you got a whole day? Because there's plenty to tell. I'll ring you. Do you have a business card?'

'Hang on.' Petra began to scrabble in her handbag and eventually pulled one out. It was embarrassingly dogeared but she handed it over.

Jeannie looked at it. 'Great. I'll be in touch.'

Finn led her out to his car, holding on to her the entire time as he steered her down the steps.

'I can manage on my own, you know,' she told him.

'I'm sure you can, but let me help you just in case.'

She turned her head and stared at him, hard. Was he mocking her? If he was, however, he gave no sign of it.

Once she was securely belted into her seat — something else Finn had done for her, his face and gleaming eyes disturbingly close to hers — she gazed through the side window at the six people watching her. Judith's face still resembled a smacked backside. For a second, Petra was sorely tempted to stick her tongue out at her. Of course, she didn't. That would be just too childish. Instead, as Finn began to steer the car along to the exit and then onto the road, she said, 'I don't think Judith liked me.'

'I wouldn't worry about that. There aren't many people Judith does like.'

'Well, I think she likes you.' She gave a small giggle, at the same time slanting a provocative glance at him.

He looked back at her, his expression suddenly hooded and impenetrable. 'Well, we've all been friends for a long time, so . . .'

'No, I didn't mean that way. I mean she obviously has the hots for you.'

Finn didn't answer straight away. He also didn't look at her. Instead, he concentrated on the road ahead. 'And what about you?' he finally and softly asked. 'Do you have the hots for me?'

She didn't stop to think twice before she replied, 'I sure do,' only to realise what it was she'd heedlessly admitted. She clapped her hand over her mouth.

He did look at her then, his eyes dancing with laughter. 'Well, they do say alcohol removes our inhibitions and releases our true emotions, so as I've got the hots for you, big time, I'd say we're on to a winner.'

Petra couldn't believe what she'd just done. 'Well, when I say I've got the hots . . . ' Frantically, she struggled to come up with an explanation for her indiscretion, only to find she couldn't.

His eyes darkened then as he looked away from her, and they didn't speak again until he was turning off the main road into the lane that led to her cottage. He pulled up at the end of her driveway and, turning off the engine, swung to face her.

'Thank you for coming out with me, Petra. I've really enjoyed it.' His eyes gleamed at her through the darkness as he unsnapped his seat belt. There were no street lights this far from town. 'I hope you did too.'

'Yes, I did. I like your friends.' She was gabbling now as she struggled with trembling fingers to unfasten her seat belt.

'Here — let me.' And he leaned across her to unclip the belt. As he did so, he swung his head to look at her, his face a mere inch from hers.

Her breath snagged in her throat as his male scent filled her nostrils and his head moved towards hers. She closed her eyes, waiting for the inevitable, and when his lips met hers, his kiss was unmistakably urgent; demanding. Petra couldn't help herself. She instinctively responded, her hands sliding up his chest to rest on his shoulders as her mouth parted beneath his. With their tongues tangling, her hands inched round to the back of his neck, where her fingers wound themselves in amongst the silky-smooth strands of his hair.

He softly groaned as he lifted his hand to the back of her head, supporting her, gently pressing her backwards, placing her in the perfect position for his mouth to roam, gently, tenderly, over her face as he kissed her closed eyelids, her cheeks, then moved on down over her arched throat, to find the tiny pulse that throbbed so tumultuously at the base. His other hand had found its way beneath her open jacket, his fingertips gently grazing her breast, touching her, caressing her, making every nerve ending that she possessed leap crazily, leaving her quivering with passion and need.

Then, as suddenly as he'd started making love to her, he stopped. He lifted his head and looked at her. 'Come on. I'll see you to the door.'

Petra stared at him. His curt words were the last things she'd expected.

'Um — do you want to come inside?'

Once again, he looked into her eyes. 'I'd better not,' he huskily told her.

'Wh-why not?'

'Things will very quickly get out of hand.'

There was no mistaking his meaning. He'd make love to her.

'Oh.'

'Yes — oh.'

'Okay. Well, thank you for tonight

and also for helping me get a van.'

'That's okay.'

'Um — about the van. It was very cheap. Did you . . . ?'

But he cut her off, his tone a brusque one. She couldn't believe that this was the same man who'd just kissed her so passionately. 'I've got several contacts who could help you.'

But she hadn't missed the fleeting look of almost alarm on his face, and she knew for certain then that he'd contributed financially to the cost.

He instantly climbed from his seat to stride round and open her door. In stunned silence, Petra got out and together they walked to her door. Once there, she pulled her door key from her handbag and, with trembling fingers, tried in vain to fit it into the lock. In the end, Finn held out his hand and she placed the key in it. He deftly unlocked the door before turning to her and saying, 'I'll be in touch.' He then swung around, and without a backward glance, strode to his car, whereupon he made a speedy U-turn and disappeared back the way they'd come.

Inside, Petra made her way slowly up the stairs, Kelly whining at her heels, as equal measures of disappointment and frustration gripped her. But her main emotion, she conceded, was that of rejection.

It wasn't till she got to the top landing that she realised what Kelly was trying to tell her.

'Oh, good Lord, you need a walk.'

She turned and walked back down. She then opened the front door and, grabbing a jacket, followed the dog outside.

'It's only going to be a quickie,' she said.

Kelly was clearly in agreement with that sentiment, because she did what she had to do and hastened back inside.

★ ★ ★

The following morning, Petra awoke to blue skies and brilliant sunshine. Sadly,

194

that didn't stop her head aching with the after-effects of the wine she'd drunk and her lingering sense of rejection. No wonder Finn hadn't wanted to stay. She'd drunk far too much. What had she been thinking of? She sighed. She'd put her weakness down to not only the stress of being with Finn but also the strain of meeting people she didn't know — particularly Judith. The wretched woman had maintained her scrutiny of her throughout the entire evening, visibly convinced she knew her; had met her before. Petra could only pray she didn't recall exactly where she'd seen her previously. It could only have been those wretched newspaper photographs. After all, they'd been plastered over every front page for days.

In an attempt to distract herself from these disturbing reflections, she said, 'Come on, Kelly, let's have breakfast and go for a good, long walk. We'll end up in the town and I'll treat myself to a coffee. Maybe Debs will join us if she's on her break.'

So the two of them once more went up to the headland, where they could eventually turn onto a road that would lead back into Poltreath. It was a long walk, but one that Petra enjoyed. Normally they only ever saw one or two people, although with summer upon them, there might be more today, especially as it was Sunday.

And she was swiftly proved right, because the first two she saw were the very ones she'd hoped to avoid. Isobel and Tara. Tara, as usual, looked as if she wanted to be anywhere else but where she was, her expression one of sulky boredom.

Determined to make one last attempt to appease Isobel, Petra cheerfully hailed them. 'Hi. Lovely morning, isn't it?'

'No,' Tara instantly muttered, 'it's just a bit of sun.' Although she did regard Kelly with a tad more interest. 'Is this the stray? She doesn't look like a stray.'

'Well, not now, no,' Petra laughed.

196

'But you should have seen her to start with.' She glanced at Isobel. The older woman's expression was closed off and almost as sulky as her granddaughter's. Nevertheless, Petra asked, 'Going to the art gallery on Thursday, Isabel?'

'Of course. One has to persevere to get anywhere, wouldn't you say?'

Petra nodded. 'I'm going to try and be there, but as I said, I'm going to be busy from now on.'

'So you did. Still, it must have made a pleasant change from your — decorating work?'

'Just a bit.'

'So how's that going?'

'Well, I haven't actually started yet. I'm still searching out materials.'

'But you must have been successful before, in Worcestershire?' Without giving Petra the chance to answer, she went on, 'Did your husband help you?'

'No, he had his own business.'

'What did he do?'

She could feel Isobel's eyes boring into her. 'Look, I must get on. Sorry, but I've so much to do.'

'Of course you have. A busy woman like you. It quite puts the rest of us to shame.' Her tone was one of spiteful sarcasm.

'Gran, can we go too — ple-ease?' Tara whined.

All Petra could do was say goodbye and walk away. Even so, she was uncomfortably aware of Isobel's gaze following her. But, really, what was the woman's problem? Other than the fact that Petra refused to divulge intimate details of her life in Worcestershire. She was obviously suspicious of her, as well as — well, envious, maybe? Envious of the fact that Petra was about to resurrect her business? While she was stuck with a depressed daughter and a hostile teenager, and struggling finan-cially, to boot.

Petra made a decision. She'd give the art class a miss for a while. Even if that did seem to be allowing Isobel to win.

★　★　★

Once she and Kelly reached Poltreath, they headed for the gallery. As it was the start of the summer season, all the shops were open despite the fact that it was Sunday, and the gallery was one of them. But before they could reach it, she saw Debs walking towards her.

'Hello, you two.' Debs crouched down and began to fondle Kelly. She glanced up at Petra. 'D'you fancy a coffee?'

'That's what I was on my way to ask you. We were going to go to the Seagull.'

'Great. Let's go, then. I've closed for coffee. Shouldn't be a problem. There haven't been any customers so far.'

Once they were settled at a table by the window and had been brought their coffees, Debs asked, ''So how are things going? I presume you got the Hogarth order?'

'I did, thanks to you. I've been there again, just to clear up a few final details. They're such a great couple.'

'They are. I'm so pleased for you, Petra.'

'Thanks. It's a huge job, though.' She grimaced. 'I just hope I'm capable of managing it.'

'I'm sure you are.' Debs eyed her over the rim of her cup. 'Have you seen the gorgeous Finn again?'

'Yes. He arrived as Elizabeth and I were discussing things. He actually helped me buy a van.'

'What do you mean, helped you buy a van?' Avid curiosity glittered at Petra.

'Well, I need one to transport all my working equipment and he knew of a reasonably priced one, so he took me along to see it. It was perfect, so I bought it. It was very cheap — a bit too cheap.' Her conviction that he'd paid something towards it hadn't lessened. Neither had her determination to repay him.

'Wow. That was beyond the call of duty.' Debs scrutinised her even more keenly now. 'He obviously likes you. Really likes you, by the sound of it.' She rolled her eyes suggestively.

'Will you stop it?' What would Debs

say if she knew she'd been out to dinner with him? She'd better keep that morsel to herself. Or at least try to. As it was, she suspected that the reddening of her face might have given the game away.

'Okay — if you insist.' But Debs continued to stare at her, gimlet-eyed now. 'But has he asked you out?'

Petra couldn't bring herself to lie. Mainly because she was so useless at it. 'Um — we-ell . . .'

Debs gave a squeal. 'He has, hasn't he?'

Petra, conceding defeat, nodded.

'Come on, woman. I want details, every last one.'

Knowing she couldn't wriggle out of it, she blurted, 'He took me to a friend's house for dinner last night.'

'Blimey. What friends?'

Petra told her.

'You jammy beggar. All I'll say is you're certainly mixing in the right circles for more work.' Debs eyed her gleefully. 'So how did that go?'

'Fine. I liked Jeannie and Rosie and

their husbands, but one woman, Judith somebody — I don't think Jeannie mentioned her surname — anyway, she was super critical. Scornful of me and all I'm doing.'

'That'll be Judith Markham. A right bitch. Is of the opinion she's superior to everyone else. Don't know why. I don't think she's ever worked at anything in the whole of her life. I can't think of a single person who likes her.'

'Yeah, that's the one.'

'I did hear that there was something going on between her and Finn at one time. But it was probably just gossip.'

Well, that would certainly go some way towards explaining her hostile attitude, Petra decided. But she'd thought better of Finn. To have an affair with a married woman — if she had been married at the time, that was? Maybe she hadn't been. But despite that, all she could think was thank goodness she hadn't agreed to a relationship with him. He clearly wasn't a man to be trusted. But just to make sure of that, she asked, 'Would that have been while she was married?'

'I don't think so.' Debs frowned. 'It was a good few years ago. Anyway, enough of that. Presumably he drove you there and back?' Her eyes were glittering eagerly once again.

'Yes.'

'And?'

'And nothing,' Petra told her. There was no way she was telling anyone what had actually happened. Not even Debs.

But she soon realised she hadn't got away with that. For Debs was eyeing her with deep scepticism. 'Nothing? He obviously fancies you if he asked you out and took you to meet his friends.'

'Apparently, he doesn't. So can we talk about something else?'

*   *   *

The rest of Sunday passed uneventfully. Petra heard no more from Finn, so he'd obviously changed his mind about her.

A conclusion which left her thoroughly dispirited.

She was thankful when Monday came round and she could embark upon her purchase of all the materials she'd need to start work. When Wednesday arrived, she called for a taxi and went to collect her van. To her relief, she drove it back to Poltreath without difficulty. She'd half expected Finn to ring her and offer his services once more. When he didn't, she decided to forget all about him. As he clearly had her.

However, so pleased was she with her driving skills, she decided not to return home but to divert into the town instead. She needed a few groceries, so this was an opportunity to get them. Which meant she was in the bakery when Jenny shared some surprising news.

'Have you heard?' she asked, her voice quivering with excitement.

'Heard what?' Petra invariably felt nervous whenever anyone asked her that, in case it was connected to her own troubles.

'Tom's turned up,' Jenny cried.

'Has he?'

'Yesterday morning. He wandered into a police station in Plymouth. Said he was lost and could they help him.' Jenny's voice softened with compassion. 'Eventually he managed to tell them his name. He was in a dreadful state. He'd got no money, his clothes were filthy and tattered, and he was starving. He'd obviously been living rough. They eventually contacted the Cornish police and transported him back here. He's in hospital — Truro — at the moment, having some sort of treatment.'

'Isobel must be hugely relieved.'

'She's beside herself, I've heard. But he's not at all well. Terribly thin, dehydrated, drifting in and out of consciousness. He's going to be moved somewhere else in due course. He needs help — mentally,' she whispered, although there was no one else in the shop to overhear. 'I haven't seen Isobel, but apparently it's resurrected all that happened, and her neighbour says she's ranting about that fraudster, thief, ratbag, whatever you want to call him. She's vowing revenge, although how she's going to get that I've no idea, seeing as he's dead. He had a lucky escape, if you ask me.' She glanced at Petra, who was staring at her in stricken silence. 'Are you okay?'

'Oh yeah, I'm fine. It's poor Isobel I'm sorry for.'

'I know. The man should have been locked up. I don't know why they don't find and arrest that wife of his. She's disappeared, apparently. Probably living the high life in some offshore tax haven, scot free, while poor Tom and Isobel are verging on destitute. In my view, someone should pay.'

'Look, I'm going to have to go,' Petra put in. She couldn't listen to any more. If only people knew. She was miles away from a life of luxury.

'Are you okay?' Jenny again asked. 'You're ever so pale. You don't know someone who's suffered the same way, do you?'

'No, no. I'm just tired, that's all. I've had a busy week, getting ready for Monday. It's all been a bit stressful.'

'Monday?'

'Yes, I begin work for the Hogarths at their house.'

'Oh, yeah. Debs told me you'd got the job. Good for you. I hope it all goes well.'

'Thanks.' Petra gave a wan smile. 'So do I. If you should see Isobel, pass on my good wishes for her and Tom.'

'Why don't you phone her? I'm sure she'd love to hear from you.'

'Um — I won't. I expect she's inundated with well-wishers calling. I'll drop her a note instead.'

'Okay, whatever you think is best. I'll see you, then.'

Petra all but ran to the door, so eager was she to get away. But all she could think was — Isobel was ranting, and not only about Grant, but about her as well. Supposing she tried to find out where Grant's wife was in order to exact the revenge that Jenny had mentioned? If she put her all into the search, she'd quickly arrive at the truth. Everything was online nowadays, newspaper archives, everything; and if Isobel should delve back to February, she'd find the photos, and then it wouldn't take much of a leap to identify Petra as Alicia Cornell. Maybe she should leave Poltreath and go somewhere else? But the same thing could happen there. Sadly, there were people all over the UK who'd been cheated out of most of their pensions.

* * *

By the time Thursday evening arrived, she felt so low in spirits that she decided she would attend the art group. Anything to distract her from her ongoing misery. She didn't think Isobel would be there, which would make her situation a whole lot easier.

The first person she encountered

when she got to the gallery was Marcus, and even that felt like a relief. He once again set up his easel alongside of her and from that moment on talked practically nonstop, mainly about Tom's reappearance, which Petra didn't really welcome but felt powerless to halt.

It wasn't until everyone was packing away their painting things that he said, 'I've been thinking about you a lot. I didn't manage to talk to you very much last week. So I wondered — how about us going out one evening? I know you said you were going to be too busy for evenings out, but I was hoping you'd make an exception for me, now that you've had the chance to think it over.'

'I can't. I really don't have the time, Marcus.'

'Honestly? All your time taken up with Finn Hogarth, is it? You found the time for him,' he snapped. 'Oh yes, I saw you with him on Saturday night —' He was regarding her with utter contempt. ' — driving in state. I just hope you know what you're doing, but that's your affair,' he sneered. 'I also hope that he doesn't treat you as he's treated dozens of other women. But if he does, don't come crying to me because you'll get no sympathy. I won't be a second choice for anyone, not even you. But one thing I can assure you of, you'll bitterly regret turning me down. In fact, you'll regret ever having come here in the first place.' And he turned away from her to angrily gather up his belongings before striding to the door and leaving the room.

Petra stared after him. What had he meant, she'd bitterly regret turning him down and regret ever coming here in the first place? He'd sounded as if he too was out for revenge. But what for? Her rejection of him in favour of Finn — a bit extreme, surely?

But he was too late, in any case. She was already wishing she hadn't come here. Wishing, in fact, that she'd never ever heard of Poltreath.

10

Monday couldn't come round quickly enough for Petra, although the sentiment was tempered by stubbornly lingering misgivings about her ability to complete such a huge task.

Eventually, of course, it did arrive. She'd taken the precaution of loading everything she'd need for the first few days into her van the evening before; all she had to do now was leave the house and drive to Greystones.

So, making sure Kelly had plenty of food and water, and promising to return at lunchtime to give her a walk, she left the house and went out to her van.

And it was then that time stopped as she stared down at four flat tyres, slashed tyres she saw upon closer examination, effectively rendering the van impossible to drive.

She gave a moan of despair.

It couldn't all be going to happen again — here, could it? She'd been so sure she'd left this kind of thing behind her; that she was about to start a new life. A life free from fear and intimidation.

But was she maybe overreacting, the shock making her think irrationally? Making her leap to the wrong conclusion entirely? Wasn't it more likely to be a few local youths getting up to mischief? There was little else for them to do here, after all. But as much as she longed to believe that, she couldn't. The damage done was too reminiscent of the things that had gone before. All those awful things that she so desperately wanted to forget.

Which had her wondering whether it could be someone from Compton Green who had traced her here, even though she'd changed her name and her appearance. She'd told no one other than her family where she was going, and she didn't think they would have passed that information on, no matter how they felt about her now.

Of course, another candidate for the damage done was Isobel. A much stronger candidate, in fact, taking into account all that Jenny had told her about Tom's misfortune and Isobel's desire for revenge. Maybe the other woman's fury had led her to embark upon that online search for information, for photographs, and she now knew who Petra really was? It could explain her unexpected malice towards Petra. It seemed more logical than mere resentment at Petra resurrecting her business.

And then there was Marcus to be considered. She recalled his words as she'd left the gallery on Thursday, that she'd regret turning him down; regret coming here. Could it be that there was no more to it than that? Plain old spite because she'd rejected his invitation? But would he really go as far as slashing tyres? Looked at rationally, it seemed unlikely.

She gnawed at her bottom lip. The truth was, it could have been anyone, anyone at all. Vandals, Isabel, Marcus, someone from Compton Green. Maybe even a stranger who, quite by chance, had recognised her in passing and subsequently discovered where she was living, possibly by tailing her back to the cottage.

But all of that aside, her main concern at this moment was the question of how she was going to get to Greystones. What a wretched start to her first job, on her very first day. What sort of impression would it give to not turn up? She supposed she could swap things over to her car, She wouldn't get it all in, but . . . She rolled her eyes at her own stupidity. How was she going to do that? Her car was in the garage, right behind the van which was blocking the driveway.

She did the only thing she could: she rang Elizabeth and apologised profusely before explaining exactly what had happened. Elizabeth gasped in shock.

Which, although she hadn't considered her as a possible candidate for the vandalism, did seem to rule her out.

'Who would do such a thing?'

'Exactly what I've been asking myself,' Petra grimly replied.

'Look, Petra dear, don't worry about being late starting. You get your van sorted out and then when you're able to, come along. The work's not urgent. We've got plenty of time.'

So that was what Petra did. She rang the local garage, and when she explained the difficulty and the urgency of having new tyres fitted, a very understanding man said, 'I'll get to you as soon as I can.' Even so, it was after four o'clock before he arrived.

After which, although he worked remarkably quickly, Petra decided it was too late to make a start at Greystones. She rang Elizabeth again. 'I'll be there tomorrow morning — definitely. I'm so sorry.' All she could do then was pray the same thing didn't happen that night too.

'Right.' She turned to Kelly. 'How

about a walk?' Anything to take her mind off her worries and fears, which were intensifying by the second.

Within minutes they were leaving the house and heading into town; she'd feel safer with people about. Not that she seriously thought she herself was in any danger.

Even so, she couldn't help thinking the damage to the van would have been a relatively easy thing for someone to do. And Isobel only lived a short way away. She could have walked here before it was light, done the deed, and returned home with no one the wiser. But, even to her, the notion was preposterous.

The first person she encountered was Jenny. But she had a hot date and wanted time to prepare herself, so they only exchanged a few words. Next came Debs. She was on her way home, but did stop for a chat.

'I thought you'd have started the Hogarth job by now,' she said.

'I intended to, but when I went out

to the van this morning, it was to find four slashed tyres. So . . . '

Debs cried, 'Who on earth would have done that?'

'Kids, maybe, with nothing better to do?' She shrugged. 'Anyway, I've had four new tyres fitted, so I can make a start tomorrow.'

And then, as if she hadn't had a bad enough day, that evening Finn showed up. She couldn't believe it when her bell rang and she opened the front door to see him crouched on her driveway, closely examining the van tyres.

'Oh, it's you.'

Finn stood up. 'Well, I've had warmer welcomes,' he said, his expression hardening. 'My mother told me what had happened, so I thought I'd call round and offer my help. But I see you've had new tyres fitted, so no problem. Other than the fact that someone deliberately slashed them.' He studied her more closely then. 'Are you all right? You don't look too good. In fact, you look extremely stressed.'

'Well, yes — a bit. It was a setback when I couldn't start work.'

'Any idea who the culprit might be?'

She shrugged. 'Local kids, probably, up to mischief.'

He did a double-take. 'Really? Why would kids do such a thing? And it's a bit more serious than mere mischief-making, taking a knife to someone's tyres. Unless they had a particular grudge, of course. You haven't had a run-in with anyone, have you?'

'No.' Why couldn't he let the matter drop? 'Look — I'm fine.'

'Have you called the police?'

'It didn't seem worth it, and when all's said and done, what can they do — or even be willing to do, come to that?'

'They'd give you a crime number to reclaim the cost of new tyres from your insurance company. Such things aren't cheap.'

Petra bit at her bottom lip. Oh God, she hadn't thought about that. She'd been so intent on getting replacements fitted as quickly as she could in order to get to Greystones. It was almost certainly too late now that she'd had new ones fitted.

'Aren't you going to invite me in?'

'Oh, um — I'm not exactly dressed for company.' She indicated her jeans and T-shirt, her usual working garb.

'That's okay.' His gaze raked her, making her embarrassingly aware of her figure hugging T-shirt. 'I'm not picky.' He gave a rakish grin. 'In fact, I like my women in casual clothes.'

'Your women?' she said indignantly. 'I'm not one of your women.'

He didn't respond to that, apart from a certain gleam to his eye; a gleam which had her wondering whether she'd made a mistake on Saturday evening and he had genuinely feared he'd lose control. In other words, he hadn't been rejecting her; he'd been protective of her. Her pulses raced as her heart thumped.

'Maybe not, but surely I deserve a drink after rushing round here to make sure you're okay?'

All of a sudden, he looked roguish and very, very sexy. Petra experienced an emotion then that felt dangerously close to desire. It flooded through her, along with the memory of the kiss they'd shared. But he was right. The least she could do was offer him a drink.

Wondering if she might be playing with fire, but unable to resist the temptation, she said, 'Okay, come in,' before turning to lead the way into her sitting room. She indicated one of the two armchairs. 'Please, sit down.'

He did so. Kelly promptly squatted at his feet. He stroked her head and then glanced up at Petra to say with a gleam of amusement, 'See, I'm not so bad. Kelly likes me. You should always trust a dog's instinct.'

'Hmm, not so sure about that,' she murmured. Although Kelly was by now nuzzling her nose into the palm of his hand. She rolled her eyes. Did he manage to win over all the females he encountered so easily? She wouldn't be surprised. She gave a muted snort of exasperation as she watched her dog. The annoying thing was that that particular sentiment turned out to be as much with herself as with Kelly. After all, she'd succumbed to his kisses pretty damned quickly. Embarrassingly quickly, as she recalled.

'So, what can I get you?'

'A glass of red wine would be perfect.'

'Merlot?

'Great. Thank you.'

She went into the kitchen and pulled a bottle from her small and now completely empty wine rack. She then opened a drawer, and with one hand, noisily riffled through the contents in the hope of somehow locating a corkscrew.

'Wow! Are you able to find anything in there?'

It was Finn. He'd followed her and was now standing immediately behind, looking over her shoulder at the jumble of items in the drawer, and close enough that she could inhale his scent.

Taking a deep breath, she swung to face him, triumphantly holding up the corkscrew which she'd managed to locate. The trouble was, he was even closer to her than she'd realised. In fact, he was so close, her breasts were touching him. She couldn't move; all she could see were the silvery-grey eyes that were staring directly into hers. Which meant she saw the exact second they narrowed and darkened. Without looking away, he took the corkscrew from her and then the bottle. Petra continued to watch as his face paled and his breathing quickened.

He replaced the corkscrew on the worktop, and then slowly unscrewed the metal cap of the wine bottle. Her breath hissed between her clenched teeth. And there she'd been, frantically hunting for the corkscrew when she hadn't even needed it. She looked up at him. Dark eyes glittered at her. She felt her face flame in embarrassment.

'Don't look so upset. It's a mistake we've all made at some time or other. Now, where are your glasses?'

Thankful for the opportunity, she turned away from him and opened a cupboard door to extract two wine glasses and place them on the worktop. He deftly poured the wine and then passed one of the glasses to her. She quickly took a large gulp.

'That thirsty, eh? Or am I making you nervous?'

He was more than making her nervous; he was practically sending her into a tailspin. Every nerve ending in her body was quivering with anticipation as she wondered whether he would kiss her again.

'No.' She wriggled past him, trying very hard to disregard the brushing of their bodies as she did so. But to her satisfaction, she heard his sudden harsh intake of breath.

She led the way back into the sitting room, where Kelly was asleep. Huh,' she grunted, 'great guard dog she is.'

'Well, she obviously realises I'm totally trustworthy.' Finn's smile was only just short of smug. 'So why don't you relax too?'

'Right. And go to sleep as well, no doubt.'

The second she saw his expression change, she knew she'd said the wrong thing. She silently groaned. He wouldn't let that remark pass, for sure.

And she was absolutely right. His grin widened into one of utter delight. 'Is that an invitation?' Desire blazed at her then, unmistakable and utterly irresistible.

Somehow, though, she managed to say, 'No, it is not.'

He pulled a wry face. 'Shame.' And he lifted his glass and took a mouthful of wine, eyeing her with unabashed lust over the rim.

Was there no stopping this man? Clearly not. Still staring at her, his eyes smouldering with — what? Desire, passion? — he took his seat, not in the armchair as she had initially indicated, but on the settee. He relaxed back into the cushions, lifting one leg to rest his ankle on the other knee, the very image of relaxed composure.

Whereas Petra, making a great show of sitting in the armchair opposite him, was jumpy and on edge, not knowing what to expect. Justifiably. Because the minute she settled herself, she felt Finn's smouldering eyes upon her. Her own stomach lurched in response and her pulses went haywire.

Not removing his gaze from her, he placed his half empty glass onto the low table between them. Petra took another large gulp of her own wine. At this rate, she was going to be drunk — again. What was this man doing to her? And why did he have to be so bloody handsome, so — bloody sexy?

But when he murmured, 'Come here. You're too far away over there. I want you close to me,' she closed her eyes, praying for the strength of will to resist him. She wouldn't be able to bear it if, after leading her on, he rejected her again. She snapped her eyes open, and desperate for any help she could get, she hurriedly swallowed another mouthful of wine.

Finn stood and strode across to her, removing the glass from her fingers, setting it on the table alongside his. He then took hold of her hand and pulled her to her feet, straight into his arms.

'You know how much I want you, don't you?' he murmured, burying his face in her hair, gently nibbling her earlobe, dropping small kisses upon the side of her face, her neck — his lips soft and warm, his breath feathering her skin as he spoke. Seductively so. 'I certainly demonstrated it the last time we were alone together.'

'And-and yet you left — as fast as you could.' Her voice was cold; accusing.

He drew back and looked at her in silence for a long moment. 'Only because I was losing control — and frankly, I wasn't sure whether it was the wine you'd drunk that was responsible for your willingness to . . . '

'To — what?'

'To make love.'

'Are you saying I was drunk?' Which, God help her, she couldn't deny.

'No, not drunk, but not totally in control. I don't take advantage of women under those circumstances.'

Petra had no answer to that other than to blurt, 'I was not drunk.'

She watched him as his air of confidence evaporated and uncertainty replaced it.

'Oh God, Petra,' he moaned, once more pulling her close and burying his face in her hair, 'do you have any idea how much I want you?'

She said nothing. He pulled her even closer, and moving his head to one side, he rested his lips on hers; softly, gently, lovingly. Petra found herself helpless against the surge of passion and desire that swamped her. They were so close she could feel his arousal. He gave a low groan and deepened the kiss, bending her backwards over his arm, forcing her lips apart and sliding his tongue inside.

Petra felt as if she was on the verge of passing out then. His kiss was a hundred times more passionate than the last time. She felt his hands move over her, tracing the curves of her body, sliding down over her hips, moulding her against him, as his other hand moved up to cradle the back of her head, holding her in position for his mouth to slide down her arched throat to the pulse that beat so madly at the base. He lingered there before continuing down into the V-neck of her T-shirt and the couple of inches of breast that it exposed. His lips explored along with his hand. His thumb lightly skimmed the peak, making her gasp aloud as passion tore through her.

But then, unexpectedly, he stopped and raised his head to look at her before swivelling them both around and walking her backwards to the settee. They dropped down together, Finn still holding her close. He pressed her onto the cushions as he resumed his lovemaking. Petra lost any desire to resist as they hungrily kissed and caressed, her heartbeat quickening until it was pulsating throughout her entire body. By this time they were lying on the settee, their desire for each other intensifying by the second. He was lifting her T-shirt over her head when Kelly gave a bark and then a throaty, rumbling growl.

That was all it took to bring Petra back to her senses. What the hell was she doing? Letting a man she'd only just met make love to her — again. Who could say he wouldn't halt things as he had last time? Leaving her aching with need? She pushed him off her and struggled to sit up, at the same time tugging her T-shirt back into place.

'Petra?' Finn looked confused and deeply, deeply frustrated. 'What's wrong?'

'Everything,' she blurted.

He blinked at her. 'Everything? I thought we were doing rather well.' He gave her a roguishly seductive grin.

'Well, that says it all,' she snapped.

His grin vanished as his eyes narrowed at her. 'Does it? Perhaps you'd care to enlighten me then, because I haven't a clue what you're talking about.'

'This — ' she scoffed, indicating the rumpled cushions, the creased covers, the clear evidence of their lovemaking, ' — isn't me.'

'Is it not?' There was a strange expression in his eyes now. 'I rather thought it was. If it's not you, who have I just been making love to?'

He was mocking her. How dare he? She leapt to her feet. Kelly only just managed to leap out of the way. 'That's right. Make fun of me . . . ' Her voice broke.

Finn, too, stood up. 'Petra, I'm not making fun of you.' His voice had softened. 'I simply don't understand.' He frowned at her. 'I thought it was rather nice.' He grinned again.

'Stop it,' she yelled, so angry was she at his — his flippancy. 'I want you to leave — now — please.'

His frown deepened. 'What? Why?'

'You took advantage.'

The frown vanished and one eyebrow shot upwards. He also was beginning to look angry. 'Took advantage of what?'

'Of me. The wine — the wine went to my head,' she stammered.

His expression then was one of scornful scepticism. 'Please, don't take me for a fool. You only had a couple of mouthfuls.'

'It was enough for me to — '

'For you to what? To show your true emotions again? Is that what's bothering you?'

'Will you please go? I'm not interested in any sort of affair — not with you.'

Kelly stood, tail hanging, ears down, as she looked from one to the other of them. She gave a soft whine.

'Oh, don't worry,' Finn's gaze was coldly contemptuous now. 'I'm going. But just because you're embarrassed at letting your barriers down — '

'I'm not embarrassed,' she snapped

back. 'I'm furious.'

'Yes, well, maybe you should decide exactly who it is you're furious with — me or yourself. But hey, I'm off.' He bent and stroked Kelly's head. 'Nice to have met you, Kelly.'

Kelly gave another soft whine and then watched, her head cocked to one side and her ears erect again, as Finn strode from the room and out of the house, and, most probably, out of their lives. Only then did Petra sit down and bury her face in her hands. What the hell had she been thinking? To allow herself to be so easily seduced? Not once, but twice. And by a notorious womaniser like Finn Hogarth? Had she no pride?

11

Despite her disgust with herself and her weakness the evening before, as well as her resolve to banish him from her mind, Petra's first thoughts the next morning were all of Finn.

She propped herself up against her pillows, her face burning at the memory of what had happened. Mainly the way she'd overreacted. Finn would have her down as yet another silly over-emotional woman. But more to the point, she had led him to believe she was a willing participant, so she must share some of the blame.

She sighed. What was the point of lying here, replaying everything? She climbed out of bed, looking round for Kelly. Her pet had taken to sleeping on the floor alongside the bed and usually waited for Petra to wake before going downstairs. She slipped on a lightweight robe and left the room, intending to go and make herself a cup of tea, as well as finding out what her pet was up to.

She'd reached the foot of the stairs before she noticed the envelope lying face down on the doormat in the hallway. Needless to say, Kelly was already there, sniffing at it. Petra bent down and picked it up. The first thing she saw was her name printed in capitals. PETRA MATTHEWS. There was no stamp, so it had been hand-delivered.

She frowned, wondering who could have done this so early in the morning. It was only just after seven thirty.

She ripped open the envelope and pulled out the single sheet of paper that was folded inside. She opened it up and read the words printed there. For an endless moment, she stopped breathing as her brain struggled to come to terms with what she was looking at.

I KNOW WHO YOU REALLY ARE, she read, and that was all.

Oh God. Just as she'd feared — no,

dreaded — someone had recognised her despite all of her precautions: changing her name, her appearance, her business, her phone, her email name and address. She'd even opened a bank account in her new name, and still someone had seen through it all to the truth.

But who? Isobel? According to Jenny, she'd been angry enough in the light of her husband's return and mental state to be vowing revenge. And how would she get that other than on Grant's wife? Her thoughts whirled giddily, until suddenly another name implanted itself into her head.

Judith. Throughout the dinner party she'd regarded Petra with deep suspicion, and she'd certainly partially recognised her. Could she have finally recalled exactly where she'd seen her before?

And then there was Elizabeth. Petra really didn't want to think it was her. The older woman already felt like a friend. Tears stung her eyes at the mere possibility. And yet, it wasn't out of the question that she'd remembered where she'd seen Petra before. In a newspaper. Petra herself had told her the name of the place she'd lived in, for God's sake. It wouldn't take much of a leap to come up with the right answer. All it would need was a search online.

And then there was Jenny. She too thought she'd seen Petra before. But if she'd remembered where and in what circumstances, wouldn't she have said something? Made some sort of accusation?

She buried her face in her shaking hands and took a deep breath.

Finally, and no matter how she tried to avoid thinking it, there was Finn. But if he'd had any idea about the details of her past and the assumptions made about her, surely he wouldn't have tried to make love to her? Or would he? Maybe he'd gambled on her being vulnerable in the wake of all that had happened. In other words, he'd viewed her as an easy conquest.

Struggling to ignore the growing nausea in the pit of her stomach, Petra walked into the kitchen and put the kettle on. A cup of good strong tea, that was what she needed. Hopefully it would calm her; help her to see things in a different light. A less scary light. It didn't, of course. An anonymous letter was an anonymous letter. Nothing was going to alter that fact.

★   ★   ★

Somehow she managed to put herself in the right frame of mind to go to Greystones. She opened the front door and somewhat nervously approached her van. Whoever had delivered the letter could at the same time have slashed her tyres again. To her overwhelming relief, she found them all intact. If it was the same person behind both things, they must have decided to leave those alone on this occasion. Maybe they'd decided an anonymous note would have more impact on her.

And with that, her sense of dread returned. Were the two incidents just the beginning? If they were, what else might whoever it was be capable of?

She heard Kelly barking and glanced back at the cottage to see her up at the kitchen window, perched on a chair, her front paws on the sill. It was as if her pet was telling her to be strong. Not to let herself be defeated. She put her hand up and waved, and then climbed into the driver's seat of the van. Life had to go on. She refused to allow whoever this was to reduce her to someone too terrified to live the way she wanted to.

She turned the ignition key and the engine fired up. All she could hope now was that Finn wouldn't be at Greystones. She simply wouldn't be able to face him after the events of the previous evening.

He wasn't. There was no sign of the Jaguar when she pulled onto the drive. Heartened by this, she climbed the steps to ring the front doorbell. Let the day begin. Work had always distracted her from her worries. She hoped it would do the same today.

Elizabeth welcomed her warmly. Nevertheless, Petra couldn't help but give her a searching look, praying she wouldn't hear the words, 'I'm sorry, but I don't want you here in my home.' But all she saw in the older woman's eyes was kindness and concern.

'Are you all right, dear? Fancy someone slashing your tyres. Do you have any idea who it might have been?'

'No, I don't. I've racked my brains, but . . . ' She shrugged. 'I've come to the conclusion it must have been local kids just making a nuisance of themselves.'

'Did Finn come to see you?' Elizabeth went on. 'He was very concerned.' She gave a knowing smile and added, 'I think he likes you.'

Petra pretended not to have heard those last few words. 'Yes, he did come. It was very kind of him.'

'He's a very thoughtful man and a wonderful son.'

Which did seem at odds with his dubious reputation.

'Anyway,' Elizabeth went on, 'I'm sure you want to get started. We've cleared the dining room ready for you.'

'That's wonderful, thank you.'

'Now, a cup of coffee before you begin?'

'I won't, thank you. I'm keen to get going after missing all of yesterday. But I would appreciate one later. I'll just go and bring my things in.'

'Okay. Eleven-ish, then, for coffee?'

'Wonderful.'

Gradually she had relaxed under the older woman's kindly gaze, and so, once she'd carried everything she'd need inside, she set about stripping the paper from the walls. It was good to get back to doing what she knew best. She'd always relished the process of transforming a room, and this would most certainly be a transformation. She'd be replacing very ordinary floral-patterned wallpaper for one of her specialist finishes: frottaging.

The existing paper came off easily and she was soon painting the ceiling. With that done, and balanced precariously halfway up the stepladder, she set about preparing the walls for the first coat of paint.

She was engrossed in her work when the door into the room opened behind her. She assumed, from the aroma of fresh coffee drifting across the room to her, that it was Elizabeth.

'I've brought you a cup of coffee.' To her horror, it was Finn, not Elizabeth.

She swivelled, to find herself looking directly over her shoulder at him with the inevitable result that she lost her balance and began to topple backwards. Despite the coffee he was holding, he was close enough to reach out with his free hand and grab hold of her, thus preventing her from falling to the floor.

'Careful,' he sharply said.

She stared at him, eyes wide, and her cheeks flaming.

He returned her stare for a moment before saying, without as much as a hint of a smile, 'I'll put it down over here, shall I?' He released his grip on her and strode to the fireplace, setting the mug on the wooden mantelpiece. He then stood, keenly inspecting the work she'd already done, a small smile finally flirting with the corners of his mouth.

'You're a quick worker, obviously,' he then told her. 'I could definitely do with your services.'

But, despite the mild words, his expression had reverted to being cold and distant. He hadn't forgiven her then for her rebuff of the evening before. Which had Petra wondering what had happened to the wonderful and thoughtful man that Elizabeth had described.

For all that, though, she heard herself saying, 'I think I need to apologise to you.'

He studied her, his surprise obvious.

'I-I think I maybe overreacted last

night,' she went on, shakily it was true, but, nonetheless she managed to say the words.

He didn't respond at first, then, 'Just a bit. It was only a kiss, after all. Well, perhaps a bit more than that, but you didn't stop me, not at first, at any rate. In fact, you gave me the distinct impression that you welcomed what I was doing.'

Stung by his low-key description of the kiss that had practically blown her mind, she said, 'Yes, well — anyway, it was a mistake.'

'Was it?' He raised the other eyebrow at her. 'It certainly wasn't on my part. It was something I'd been wanting to do — quite badly.'

Petra was forced to watch as desire flared in his eyes. However, it was only a fleeting impression, gone almost as soon as it appeared. Could she have imagined it?

'Here's an idea,' he said. 'How about we start over? Maybe it was my fault, too. I was a little . . . ' He paused. Petra held her breath, wondering what was coming next. ' . . . full on. Let's have a meal, just the two of us. It will give us a chance to get to know each other properly. I promise I'll behave.' He smiled then, a wickedly beguiling smile.

Petra wondered if any woman had ever been able to resist him. She doubted it, and she was no exception to that. But his manner towards her did reinforce her belief — hope — that the letter writer wasn't him.

'Okay,' she agreed. 'Let's call a truce, and yes, I'd like to have a meal with you.'

He made no attempt to hide his surprise, and she questioned whether she was doing the right thing. 'You're a very lovely woman, even in that rather disreputable T-shirt you're wearing.' His voice was throaty, seductive; reminding her of his lovemaking and the way he'd been well on the way to removing a similar garment the evening before. 'Very sexy — sorry, that was way over the top.'

He'd clearly detected her uncertainty.

'You have no need to worry, I can assure you of that. I'll restrain my . . . baser instincts, unless, of course,' he went on, 'you invite them.' The last three words were uttered so low she could barely hear them.

But hear them she did. 'That's highly unlikely.' She spoke through tight lips. 'But if you feel you can't . . . '

'I will be the perfect gentleman. I can be, you know, when I put my mind to it. Whatever the temptation.' This last was again said so softly, she wondered if he'd intended that she shouldn't hear him. However, she had heard, and had her mouth open to remonstrate with him when he went on, 'I'll reserve us a table at The Angel, shall I?'

'The Angel?' From what she'd heard, that was the most exclusive as well as the most expensive restaurant in the area. A piercing excitement stabbed her. It had been so long since she'd been wined and dined by a handsome man. She didn't count their last meal together; they'd been just two amongst eight. This would be different; more intimate. Uncertainty once more flickered in the wake of that notion. Was that what she really wanted? Could she trust him?

'Have you been?' he asked.

'No, I-I'm not sure I have the right clothes.' She glanced down over herself. 'As you can see.'

Amusement toyed with the corners of his mouth as his glance followed hers down. 'Well, maybe not those particular clothes, but it's smart casual, nothing too formal. Just be yourself.'

'I'd prefer to be dressed,' she riposted.

He laughed then, really laughed. 'Wear whatever you're comfortable in.'

'Okay, jeans and T-shirt it is, then.' Now it was her turn to twinkle with laughter.

His face paled dramatically as he looked at her. And even his voice quivered when he spoke. 'So, sh-shall we say, seven thirty tomorrow evening?

I'll pick you up.'

And all of a sudden, she felt more confident in her ability to hold her own with him. He wasn't quite as composed around her as he liked to pretend. 'Will you get a table that quickly?'

'Oh yes. Maurice, the maître d', can always fit me in.'

I'm sure he can, Petra mused. She couldn't imagine many people having the temerity to refuse Finn Hogarth anything.

'Okay, we start over.'

'Good. So, I'll leave you to your work. You're doing a great job, by the way.'

'Thank you,' she demurely answered. 'Not that there's much to see yet.' She ignored Finn's snort of mirth as he left the room and his softly drawled words, 'Oh, I wouldn't say that.'

★   ★   ★

The rest of the day progressed well. She even managed to put the arrival of the

247

anonymous letter out of her head. She returned home at lunchtime to walk Kelly but was swiftly back again to carry on. With luck, she'd soon be able to begin the frottaging process.

By the time, she returned to Sea View Cottage that evening, a bit later than she'd planned, Kelly was sitting right inside the door, clearly desperate for a walk.

It wasn't until she moved that Petra spotted another envelope on the mat. This time, her married name was printed on the front. ALICIA CORNELL.

She stared at it for a long moment before, with a sensation of utter dread, ripping the envelope open and unfolding the single sheet of paper inside.

WHERE'S ALL THE MONEY YOU STOLE? NO ONE BELIEVES YOU DIDN'T KNOW WHAT YOUR GREEDY VILE HUSBAND WAS DOING. WE ALL KNOW YOU'RE AS GUILTY AS HE WAS AND SO YOU'RE THE ONE WHO'S GOING TO PAY. THAT'S A PROMISE.

She let the paper flutter to the floor as she staggered back and sank down onto the bottom stair. She buried her face in her hands and gave a sob of fear and despair. There it was — the first threat. And how did they intend making her pay? In actual cash, or some way more sinister? Would whoever it was physically hurt her? What was she to do? It must be someone who lived here in Poltreath. Although she'd tried not to, she'd heard quite a few people talking, naming friends and acquaintances whose pensions and jobs had been severely affected by Grant. Tom was just one of them.

As if sensing her distress, Kelly came over to her and pushed her nose between her hands, softly whining as if to ask, 'What's wrong?'

'What shall I do, Kelly? Move away, but who's to say the same thing wouldn't happen somewhere else?'

Kelly licked Petra's fingers, offering the only sort of comfort she could. She put her arms around the dog's neck and buried her face in the soft fur. 'What am I to do?' Her crying intensified, making Kelly begin to cry in her own way.

'Okay.' She dashed the tears away. 'I'm not going to be bullied like this. None of it was my fault, no matter what people think.'

For a start, why would she be living in this small cottage and about to start painting peoples' houses if she had millions of pounds at her disposal? Whoever this was must surely have realised that? They knew where she lived. She got to her feet. 'I'll wash my face and we'll go for a walk.'

Kelly stopped crying and danced around her legs. She managed a weak smile. 'What would I do without you?'

So that was what she did. She changed into clean clothes, washed her face, and then applied a fairly heavy layer of makeup. Even so, her eyes were still red-rimmed and swollen. That would fade, however. Her dread and fear wouldn't. Nonetheless, they'd go on their favourite walk, along the cliff-top path. That way, hopefully, they wouldn't see many people.

And, just as she'd hoped, they met no one. She did glimpse a couple in the distance and her step faltered for a moment, but then they branched off, heading another way. By the time the two of them returned home, they were both weary and hungry. So Petra gave Kelly her supper first and then prepared herself an omelette and salad. After watching an old episode of Vera in an effort to distract herself from her growing problems, she realised she was exhausted and took herself and Kelly off to bed.

Not surprisingly, she didn't sleep well. What she did do was dream. Nightmarish dreams, of someone threatening her, and, at times, a mob of people surrounding her, their faces full of hate as they screamed abuse at her. Marcus was amongst them, as was Isobel. Unexpectedly Jenny, Debs and Elizabeth were also there. And even Finn made an appearance, his good-looking features twisted with disgust.

They threw stones at her, chanting, 'We know who you are. We know what you did.'

In the end, she abandoned any attempt at sleep and got up. She spent the remainder of the night downstairs in the armchair, wrapped in a duvet, Kelly asleep over her feet.

12

As weary as Petra was after her practically sleepless night, her work didn't suffer. Elizabeth came into the room several times and proclaimed her satisfaction with what Petra had accomplished so far.

'I hear Finn's taking you out this evening,' she said at one point. 'To The Angel, no less.'

'Yes.' Petra put down her brush for a second. 'Maybe you could give me a bit of advice? What should I wear? I've not been there before. Finn said smart casual, but . . . ' She bit at her bottom lip. He'd said that the last time and she'd found herself way overdressed.

'We-ell, if I were you, I'd go for a dress. Keep it fairly simple and dress it up with jewellery. You can't go wrong with that. And a nice pair of shoes. How's that?'

'I have just the dress. Thank you, Elizabeth. I appreciate it.'

After that, she felt happier — well, as happy as she could be with the threat that was hanging over her. Add to that the fear that her persecutor would reveal her identity and Elizabeth — or worse — Finn would learn the truth of who she was, and it was no wonder that her insides continually churned with a deep-seated dread.

It was a relief at the end of the day to finish work and say goodbye to Elizabeth. She'd lived in constant fear that the older woman would come into the room and say, 'I know who you are'; that her anonymous letter writer would have broadcast the truth.

However, she hadn't. Instead, she smiled warmly as she asked, 'Are you off?'

'Yes, I've done all I can for today. Could you leave the windows open for a while?'

'Of course. Well, have a nice evening.' And she gave Petra a smile that this time had a hint of mischief in it. 'As I've said before, Finn likes you.'

'Has he said something, then?'

'He didn't have to. I know my son. He's never been able to fool me.'

* * *

She headed for home, turning Elizabeth's words over and over in her mind. Finn liked her. Was that why he was persevering with her? Refusing to give up?

Despite the lingering sense of dread and fear, a low-key happiness filled her as she finally admitted that she liked him too. Which meant that if he kissed her again this evening, as she was sure he would — despite his words to the contrary — she'd respond, despite knowing it could lead nowhere; not as long as she concealed her true identity.

She let herself into the cottage to be greeted by an overjoyed Kelly. 'Okay, okay,' she murmured. 'Let me have a moment and then we'll go for a walk.'

Kelly barked enthusiastically. Petra was beginning to believe the animal understood everything she said — which was crazy, wasn't it?

'And then I'll have to get ready to go out.'

The dog sat down on her haunches, cocked her head to one side, and whined softly.

'I know. I'm sorry, darling, but I won't be late, I promise.'

With their walk over, Petra went straight upstairs to pull her new dress from the wardrobe. She held it up in front of her. Was it really sophisticated enough for the sort of place she guessed The Angel would be?

She showered and shampooed her hair, blow-drying it before piling it up into a casual arrangement on the top of her head and anchoring it with several pins. She then applied her makeup and carefully slipped the dress over her head. The fabric was a soft, fine jersey and clung lovingly to her curves. Like the two-piece outfit she'd worn before, the dipping neckline revealed more of her cleavage than she remembered from her first try-on in the shop.

She rummaged through her jewellery box and dragged out a long bronze-coloured chain. It was long enough to drape round her neck a couple of times, something which she hoped would distract from the inches of flesh on display. She still had all of the jewellery that Grant had given her over the years, but she was reluctant to wear that. It could lead Finn to question how someone like her possessed pieces of such obvious value.

As she slipped her arms into a lightweight jacket and descended the stairs, the doorbell chimed.

She opened the door and there was Finn, looking devastatingly handsome in a blue shirt and beige trousers. His jacket was a deeper shade of blue than his shirt. It warmed his silvery eyes, making them look several shades darker as they skimmed all over her.

'You look gorgeous,' he breathed.

'You're not so bad yourself,' she lightly riposted.

Amusement gleamed at her. 'Good, because I aim to please.'

'Oh — you certainly do that,' she murmured under her breath.

He didn't respond to that, but she'd swear he'd heard her. There was something, a certain flicker, in his gaze that betrayed him as he asked, 'Ready?'

'Yes.' She closed the door behind her and allowed him to shepherd her into the luxurious Jaguar.

Finn started the engine and turned the car in order to follow the road back into Poltreath. The town was almost deserted as they drove through it, despite most of the shops still being open. She spotted Isobel and Tara coming out of the grocery store, Tara sporting a bad-tempered scowl as usual. Mind you, Isobel didn't look much happier. But then, she did have cause. She must be out of her mind with worry about her husband's condition. Petra couldn't help wondering, though, if her look of anxiety — misery, even — was connected to what she might possibly be doing. Blackmailing Petra. Even going so far as to threaten her.

Once they'd left the narrow street behind and turned onto the main highway, Finn picked up speed and within a very short time, they were pulling into a car park behind an impressive-looking restaurant.

It had been a long time since Petra had been anywhere quite so grand. However, her flicker of apprehension was instantly quelled by the formally dressed maître d' saying, 'So good to see you again, Mr Hogarth.' He then turned his attention to Petra, his eyes warm with admiration. 'And you, madame.'

'Thank you,' she murmured.

'This,' Finn then said, 'is Poltreath's newest resident, Maurice. Petra Matthews.'

'It's very good to meet you, Ms Matthews. Now, may I take your jacket?'

He took it from her and handed it to another waiter before ushering them to a table in a secluded corner. A small tree planted in a huge pot partially shielded them from the gazes of the other diners.

They sat down and Finn asked for a bottle of Bollinger champagne.

Maurice clicked his fingers and yet another waiter appeared to take the order. Within a couple of minutes, their glasses were being filled and Finn lifted his to his mouth, saying, 'Thank you for coming this evening, Petra.'

'Thank you for asking me,' she primly replied before taking a generous mouthful of the champagne. A huge mistake. The bubbles hit the back of her throat and then whizzed up the back of her nose, making her cough and splutter as she struggled for breath.

Finn instantly got to his feet. She flapped her hand at him, indicating he should sit back down as the spasm eased and her breathing returned to normal. 'Okay?' he asked.

'Fine. It went down the wrong way. Sorry.'

She felt very foolish, and very juvenile, a sensation emphasised by the amused manner in which a few of the other diners were regarding her. Yet, it hadn't been that long ago that she'd regularly drunk champagne. Grant had loved to flaunt his wealth and importance in a very obvious way, usually by sending back the first bottle of whatever he'd ordered and demanding another — to Petra's acute embarrassment. In the end, she'd made excuses not to go out with him, pleading pressure of work. Which only added to the distance that was developing between them.

Luckily, a waiter arrived, holding large menus so Petra could bury her flushed face behind hers as she tried to decide what to order. She plumped for a starter of crab mousse on a bed of tenderleaf salad, followed by pork medallions in a champagne and mushroom sauce with baby new potatoes.

Finn opted for smoked salmon to be

followed by a simply grilled fillet steak accompanied by a selection of vegetables, which he declared they could share. With their orders taken, he sat back in his chair and watched her across the table, his fingers lazily toying with the stem of his glass. Then he asked the question she'd been dreading. 'So — tell me about yourself. Where you lived, about your family and friends, everything.'

'There's not really much to tell you. I lived in a small village in the Midlands, ran my own business — interior decoration, of course.'

'What did your husband do?'

'Oh, lots of things. Most of which I knew very little about. He used to make regular business trips to Europe and the States. His interests were extremely diverse.'

'So what happened to them when he died?'

She hesitated. Would he recall all the newspaper stories about Grant's bankruptcy, the photographs of them both, and, against all the odds, put two and two together? Finn Hogarth, she was beginning to realise, was an extremely shrewd man, judging by the sheer amount of wealth he'd accumulated over just a few years. It wouldn't do to underestimate him. And it was only four months ago that the stories had been all over the front pages. 'They-they were taken into receivership.' She could hear the quiver in her voice. Would Finn hear it too and wonder at her sudden agitation?

He watched her for a long nerve-racking moment before asking, 'How did he die — if you don't mind me asking?'

Deciding to stick to the story she'd already told anyone who'd asked, she said, 'He'd been ill for a while, so in the end . . . ' She shrugged her shoulders, hopefully closing the topic down.

It worked, because all Finn said was, 'I'm sorry.' He tilted his head and went on, 'I presume you don't have any children?'

'No.'

'Any family?'

'I have parents, and a brother. They live in Cheshire.'

'Will you be seeing them? Are they planning to visit?'

'At some point, yes.' Again, she kept it vague. It still hurt deeply that they hadn't wanted to be associated with her in the wake of the scandal and clearly still didn't — apart from a very rare email from her mother, that was.

Finn was watching her closely. Too closely. Had she inadvertently revealed something of her distress? Quickly, she rearranged her expression. But Finn wasn't fooled.

'Is everything okay between you all? You look — well, a little unhappy, I suppose.'

'It hasn't been the best of times,' she bit back. 'I came here to try and make a fresh start.'

'And here I am, forcing you to relive it all. I'm sorry. It must have been painful for you.'

'It was, and I prefer to leave it all behind. Tell me about yourself.'

He grinned then. 'What you see is what you get. I've never been married.'

'Yes, I know.'

'Of course you do. I tend to forget what an efficient communications system we have in Poltreath.' His tone was one of dry irony. 'I've never met anyone that I would wish to spend the rest of my life with. Until . . .'

She hurriedly interrupted him. She suspected he'd been about to say 'until now'. In which case, as much as the idea that he might want to spend his life with her thrilled her, she had no idea how to respond to that. Not without telling him the truth about herself. 'What about your business interests? You're obviously very successful.'

'They're fairly varied, like your husband's. I play the financial markets, and I have a property development company; it operates both here and in the north of England. I recently acquired several manufacturing and engineering businesses, also mainly in the north. That's something I'm interested in becoming more involved with. I'm hoping to expand them, build them up into a nationwide chain. The industry has been in decline for several years now, and I'd like to have a go at resurrecting it here in the UK.' He gave a quick smile. 'Not least to encourage buying British rather than French or German. I have a partner in that. He's the expert, so I mainly leave it to him. And I'm very interested in the growth of AI, artificial intelligence,' he elaborated. 'It's going to be huge, everywhere, so I'm trying to get involved in that too.'

'Wow,' she said. 'What sort of properties do you develop?' Even to her own ears, the question sounded lame, but it was the only one she could come up with. Most of what he'd mentioned sounded very high-tech and thus very complicated. She wouldn't know where to start asking about it all.

'All sorts. We're working on a leisure

centre and hotel at the moment, a few miles out of Truro. If that goes well, I plan to expand all over the UK. We also build houses, the upper end, small exclusive gated estates. We renovate run-down properties and then let them for affordable rents. Although that's not as profitable as it used to be. So I'll probably move out of that side of things.'

She pulled a face. 'Makes me look very small fry in comparison.'

'Not at all. You're a specialist in your field, and these days there's a great deal of demand for something different; unique. In fact, I can probably give you work in the future in a new development we're planning.' He shrugged. 'Anyway, that's enough about me, and here's our food.'

Their conversation then took a more general turn, ranging from their tastes in books — they both enjoyed thrillers — to the food they liked, and how they spent their leisure time. 'Not that I have too much of that,' Finn laughed.

'You're lucky to have Kelly. It makes you get out and take some exercise, fresh air.'

'But you exercise, don't you?' Her gaze wandered to the breadth of his shoulders, the width of his chest. 'You look very fit.'

'Well, I try, but I could do more. I do play golf, when I have the time.'

Of course he did, Petra wryly reflected. What wealthy businessman didn't? Grant used to conduct a large proportion of his deals on the golf course. Or at least, that was how he'd explained the time he'd spent away from the house, when he wasn't abroad somewhere, of course. Listening to Debs complaining about her husband's absences — according to him, spent on the golf course — suspicion had turned into conviction that Grant had been with a woman, or, more likely, a succession of women. He'd been a flamboyant, handsome man, and extremely rich to boot. It would have proved a powerful attraction to a certain type of woman. As for her own feelings about him, she'd cared less and less.

Surprisingly, the evening sped by, and all too soon it was time to leave. Maurice brought Petra's jacket to her and handed it to Finn, who then helped her into it, his fingers brushing the nape of her neck, sending shivers of anticipation all the way down her spine. She couldn't help thinking — would he try to kiss her?

So, when they reached her cottage and he parked on the roadside, she was more than a little disappointed when he turned to her and said, 'Thank you, Petra. I've really enjoyed this evening, enjoyed learning more about you. Getting to know you.'

She met his gaze, her own full of anticipation, she was sure, only to see no hint of desire. 'Oh — well, so have I.' Could he detect the disappointment in her tone? If he did, he gave no indication of it. 'Thank you for taking me.'

'We'll have to do it again sometime.'

Oh Lord, that didn't sound good. Too casual, way too casual. It was akin to saying, 'See you around.' Somehow, she mustered up the requisite response. 'That would be nice.' Nice? Nice? Couldn't she come up with something more imaginative than that?

Something flickered in his eye then. Satisfaction? Had he detected her disappointment? She wouldn't be surprised. It had most likely shown on her face. The same face that now flushed pink.

'Come on,' was all he said, however. 'I'll see you to the door.'

'There's really no need. It's only a few feet away.'

'I insist.' His expression was as cool as his voice as he climbed from his seat and walked around the car to open her door and help her out.

Petra could have wept. Elizabeth was wrong. He didn't like her. He'd have tried to kiss her if that was the case. She'd ruined her chances of even a short-term relationship by rejecting him so vehemently. He was a proud man, that much was self-evident. She'd turned him down, so that was that. But if that was the case, why had he asked her out? To show her what she was missing? They walked to the front door.

'Have you got your key?'

She groped in the bottom of her handbag and then handed it to him. He took it and opened the door. She was about to step inside when he leant forward and dropped a kiss onto her cheek. She inhaled the scent of him, of his aftershave, his masculine scent. Boldly then, she tilted her head and looked directly up at him, deliberately widening her eyes.

And when she saw him take a deep breath, she knew her tactic had worked. However, he made no move to take her up on her subtle invitation, even though his narrowed eyes glinted at her through the darkness.

'Goodnight, Petra.' His voice was low and throaty.

'Goodnight,' she said, helplessly watching as he strode back to his car. Well, she sighed, that was that. Clearly she'd blown it. She went inside. Or — could he be deliberately playing hard to get? If so, it was working.

She greeted Kelly and then went upstairs to get undressed. She was way too uptight to go to bed, so she slipped into her dressing gown and returned downstairs. She'd check her emails. Her mother occasionally, very occasionally, got in touch that way, and right now she needed to know she was at least thought about, if not loved.

The laptop booted up remarkably quickly. The broadband was much faster here than back in Worcestershire. She went to her inbox and saw at once there was nothing from her mother. But there was something from an unknown account; an account with the name of Nemesis. One email.

Curiosity made her take a chance and open it. She didn't usually open anything she wasn't sure about in case it contained some sort of virus. But under the present circumstances, she couldn't stop herself. However, she quickly wished she'd resisted the temptation, because what she read had her giving a cry of sheer horror.

13

The words were once again printed in capital letters, and they sent a chill right through Petra.

YOUR HUSBAND KILLED HIMSELF AND MANAGED TO ESCAPE JUSTICE. SO, UNLESS YOU COME UP WITH THE MONEY YOU STOLE, YOU WILL BE THE ONE TO PAY THE PRICE. I'M COMING FOR YOU. BE WARNED. NEMESIS.

Petra stared at the laptop screen. Come up with the money? How the hell was she supposed to do that? All right, she had her jewellery, but even if she sold it all, there would be nowhere near enough to repay the millions Grant had stolen. She re-read the words, horrified at their implications.

This had to be a local person; someone who had taken one of the cards she'd distributed around the town. It would be a simple matter to open an email account under an anonymous name. People did it all the time.

Struggling for calm, she studied the name, Nemesis. Something about it rang a bell. Wasn't it the name of a goddess? She went in search of her Oxford reference dictionary and looked it up. She read — Nemesis, a goddess portrayed as the agent of divine punishment for wrongdoing. Of retribution. Vengeance.

She stared again at the words on the screen. This was wholly different to what had happened in Compton Green. This implied mental — if not physical — punishment of her for what Grant had done.

Her first instinct was to dial 999 and ask for the police, but they'd expect her to explain the contents of the email and reveal her true identity. And who could say that they wouldn't release that information to the press?

Kelly came to sit at her feet. She gave

several low whines.

'Yes, I know — you need to go out. I forgot. Sorry, sweetie.'

She slipped an anorak over her dressing gown and gingerly opened the door, glancing fearfully up and down the road before letting the dog run out. Kelly, oblivious to any hint of danger, wasted no time in hurrying across the road to a patch of grass. To Petra's relief, she did what she needed to and quickly returned. Not that she believed her persecutor would be outside. There was a full moon illuminating the landscape, so she'd have easily spotted anyone hanging around.

★ ★ ★

After spending another night tormented with nightmares, she decided to phone her mother before setting off for work. She needed the reassurance, the comfort, of hearing the voice of someone close. A family member. Surely it was time they put their resentment and hostility against her to rest? It wasn't as if their pensions had been affected. They hadn't worked for Grant. He'd always told her he wouldn't employ either family members or friends. It invariably caused problems. So at least he'd had some principles.

Her mother answered on the third ring. 'Mum, it's me,' she tentatively said. She couldn't be sure her mother wouldn't put the phone straight down again. When she didn't, she went on, 'I-I was wondering — d-do you and Dad fancy a holiday? I've got room and I could really do with the company. I-I miss you both.'

Her mother's tone was a warmer one than the last time they'd spoken, so that was something to be grateful for. However, the answer to her invitation didn't follow through on that. 'We can't just at the moment, love. Your dad's too busy at work. But we'll try to make it sometime soon. Promise. Sorry, I'm just about to go out.'

Disappointed and saddened by her

mother's refusal, yet buoyed by the hope she felt at the words *we'll try to make it soon, promise,* she decided she needed a distraction from her disappointment as well as her deepening feelings of dread. She set off on a brisk but not very long walk with Kelly, after which, feeling fractionally better, she headed off to Greystones, where Elizabeth was waiting for her.

'So how did last night go?'

Her expression was one of such keen anticipation that Petra felt really bad about having to disappoint her. 'Good. The food was gorgeous. Very enjoyable.' She did manage a smile, weak it was true, but a smile nonetheless.

Elizabeth made no attempt to mask her disappointment. 'Oh, I see.'

In an attempt to seem more upbeat, Petra managed another smile, a slightly warmer one this time, still giving nothing of her real emotion away, she hoped, as she lightly said, 'I think you might have misjudged Finn's interest in me.'

'No way. I know my son.' She eyed Petra. 'He's playing some sort of game. Tactics — he's very good at those.' She was still keenly eyeing Petra. 'You didn't upset him, did you?'

'I-I don't think so.' She could hardly tell Finn's mother that he'd previously tried to make love to her and on both occasions she'd knocked him back — and none too gently. Something occurred to her then. Rather than clever tactics, could his cool goodbye last night have been some sort of revenge for her rejection of him? Punishment, even? No, of course it wasn't. If she hadn't received that hateful email, she'd never have considered him being capable of such vindictive behaviour.

'He's playing hard to get,' Elizabeth confidently declared. 'I know he's keen on you. I could see it. A mother knows. He's trying to capture your interest. Intrigue you. Yes, I'm sure of it.'

But Petra wasn't anywhere near so sure, even though she herself had at one point wondered the same thing. Absent-mindedly, she took the mug of coffee that Elizabeth thrust into her hand.

'Here you are — to get you started.' She then stared hard at Petra. 'Are you feeling okay, my dear? You're looking very pale. You're not sickening for something, are you?'

'I don't think so. I hope not.' But, truth to tell, she wasn't feeling too good. She'd felt vaguely out of sorts yesterday. She'd put it down to stress. Not only the stress of starting what she suspected was going to be a difficult job, but also the stress of knowing that someone in this small town hated her enough to persecute her for something she'd had no hand in. But now, after reading that awful email, she wondered — for the umpteenth time — had someone from Compton Green somehow managed to track her down? Yet she'd told no one where she was going apart from her parents, and surely they wouldn't have passed it on to anyone else? No, it had to be someone who lived here. It was the only logical explanation.

Trying to restore some sort of equilibrium, she resolved to put the sensation of nausea and the intense headache that was now afflicting her down to a combination of fear, stress, and lack of sleep over the past few nights. A spot of hard work would soon put things right.

She took a sip of coffee, and that was all that was needed. Her stomach heaved against the powerful smell. Elizabeth was a lover of strong coffee and assumed that everyone else shared that taste. And normally Petra did. But this morning . . . She set the mug down on the worktop and groaned, 'Can I go to your loo?'

'Yes, dear, you know where it is.'

Petra dashed off and almost threw herself through the doorway to crouch over the toilet bowl, where she was very, very sick.

'Petra, dear.' It was Elizabeth. She must be standing right outside the door. 'Are you all right?'

Petra wiped her mouth with the back of her hand. 'I've been sick. I'm sorry.'

'I'm coming in, dear.'

And in the next second, Elizabeth was there by her side, holding her hair back from her forehead as she helped Petra to her feet. Then, moistening a hand towel, she gently wiped Petra's forehead and face.

'Come along, dear, into the kitchen and let's have a look at you. You can't work in this condition; you must go home.'

She led Petra into the kitchen again and helped her onto one of the breakfast-bar stools. She fetched a glass of water and stood over Petra as she sipped it.

'Right. You can't drive yourself, not feeling like you are. I'll ring Finn — I'd ask David, but he's got to go out.'

'No, please.' Horrified, Petra tried to stop her. Finn was the last person she wanted to see. She glanced down over herself. She was a mess. Her T-shirt had a suspicious stain on it, and she must be reeking of vomit.

'Or maybe you should stay here.' Elizabeth was regarding her with deep concern. 'We have the room, goodness knows, what with five bedrooms. That way, I can keep an eye on you.'

'No, I really can't. I have a dog, as you know. Kelly. I have to go home. I can't leave her.'

'Right.' Elizabeth looked determined as she pressed the speed dial button on her phone.

Petra softly groaned as Elizabeth said, 'Finn, darling, it's Mum. I've got Petra here and she's been quite dreadfully sick. She needs to be taken home — I can't take her, my car's in for service.' There was a moment's silence before she said, 'Oh, thank you, darling. She's really not fit to drive.'

She ended the call and turned back to a Petra who was feeling more ill by the second.

'He's on his way. He'll be here in five minutes.'

'That really isn't nec — ' But she couldn't complete the sentence. Instead, she was forced to make another dash for the loo, where she was once again violently and noisily sick. It was almost projectile vomiting. What the hell had caused this? Something she'd eaten? Tears stung her eyes. She couldn't bear for Finn to see her like this. But her protests, weak as they were, proved in vain. In the next moment, Finn was striding into the house.

'Where is she?'

Elizabeth said, 'In here.' She was obviously hovering just outside the door again.

To Petra's complete horror, he strode into the loo, where she was still crouched over the toilet bowl. The vomiting had mercifully stopped, for the moment at least, but she felt too weak to stand.

Finn leant over and, placing his hands under her arms, gently lifted her to her feet and straight up into his own arms, effortlessly cradling her as if she were no heavier than a child.

'No, please . . . ' she weakly protested. 'I'm smelly.'

'Hush,' he firmly told her as he carried her out of the cloakroom. 'I'll take you into the snug, where you can have a lie-down before I drive you home.'

She gazed at him in horror. Supposing she vomited all over the Jaguar's immaculate interior? Tears once again welled as he carried her into the snug and laid her on the settee. She gave a small sob.

'Can you get her some water, Mother?'

'Here — I've already got it, and a bowl, just in case.' She smiled kindly down at an ashen-faced Petra. 'Now, you do as you're told.' She smiled again in an effort to soften what was unarguably an order. 'You rest, and then Finn will take you home.'

Petra felt too weak and far too ill to argue. She relaxed back against the soft cushions and sipped from the glass of water.

'Th-thank you,' she murmured. She couldn't bring herself to look at him for fear of what she'd see in his eyes. Disgust, most probably. Revulsion? Yes, that would be the one.

'Petra,' he quietly said, 'look at me.'

Reluctantly, she did. She was too weak for an argument of any sort. But instead of the disgust and revulsion she'd anticipated, she saw only compassion and tenderness. It was at that point that the tears overflowed and ran down her wan face.

'I'm so sorry,' she sobbed. 'I don't want to be any trouble.'

'You're not. Now, here's what's going to happen. You're going to rest right where you are for a while, and then I'll drive you home. I'll stay there with you until you feel better. Mother — ' He swivelled his gaze to Elizabeth. ' — once we've gone, can you get a taxi to the manor and bring me a couple of changes of clothes? Bring them to Sea View.'

Horror again engulfed Petra at the

idea of Finn staying with her. 'You don't need to do that. I can manage.'

He looked down at her. 'I really don't think you can. I'm not leaving you alone while you're obviously so ill. End of story.'

'I've got Kelly.'

'Oh yes, Kelly will make a splendid nurse. I can just see her carrying glasses of water up the stairs, emptying the sick bowl.' He grinned down at her. 'I'll make a much better nurse, so there's no point in arguing. My mind is made up.'

Petra stared appealingly at Elizabeth, but all she got in return was a very satisfied and ever so slightly smug smile. They were ganging up on her.

★ ★ ★

All of which meant that as soon as Petra's nausea lessened, Finn escorted her to his car, reclined the seat before draping a blanket over her legs, and drove her back to Sea View.

Kelly, for once, made no sound; she

simply followed Finn as he helped Petra up the stairs. He'd have lifted her up into his arms if she hadn't protested that she could manage. Nevertheless, he had to practically lift her up over the last two stairs.

'Which door?' he asked when confronted by three of them. Well, five if you counted the storage cupboards.

'The furthest one,' she murmured.

He headed for that and, as it was standing open, he guided her straight in, keeping his arm about her waist, taking her full weight as if he were carrying something no heavier than a bag of sugar. He helped her to the bed, and with one hand pulled the duvet back ready for her to climb in.

'Okay. Now where do I find clean — ' He stared at her. 'What do you wear in bed?'

'An old T-shirt, usually. In the top drawer of the chest.'

He sat her on the bed and went to it. He pulled out a T-shirt and carried it back to her. Petra sat, paralysed with horror. He wasn't going to undress her, was he?

A smile flirted with the corners of his mouth. 'Don't look so alarmed. I'll turn my back while you change. Unless, of course — ' His smile widened into a grin. ' — you want me to help?'

'Certainly not,' she bit back, albeit weakly still. 'I can manage perfectly well.' Which she did. Nonetheless, she kept her eyes on him, making sure he didn't swivel his head in her direction. Once she'd undressed, she hurriedly climbed into bed and tugged the duvet up over her.

'Are you decent yet?' She could tell by his tone that he was still grinning.

'Yes.'

He swung round then and strode to the bed. He proceeded to tuck the duvet tightly around her and made sure her pillows were comfortably positioned before declaring, 'Right. I'll get you some water, and then I would suggest you try and sleep. In my view, that's the best remedy of all.' He scrutinised her closely. 'If you should feel sick, shout. I'll come up.'

He then turned and left the room, Kelly at his heels. He was back in a remarkably short time, holding a jug of water, a glass, a towel and a bowl. 'In case you can't make it to the bathroom. Do you have a doctor here?'

'No, I haven't got round to registering yet.'

'I'm going to ring my own doctor, then. He can give you the onceover.'

'There's absolutely no need,' she protested. 'I'll be fine . . . ' But as if to prove her wrong, the nausea surged yet again. She reached for the bowl, past caring by this time that Finn would be witness to the disgusting sight. Which was just as well, because she vomited over and over, wrenching her stomach and hurting her throat.

And throughout it all, Finn sat by her side, one hand gently rubbing her back until she fell back, exhausted, against the pillows, every vestige of colour drained from her.

'That does it. I'm calling the doctor.' And, pulling a mobile phone from his pocket, he did just that. 'He's coming straight round.'

She stared at him. Did the man not have any other patients to see? It was either that, or Finn had one hell of an influence over him.

Whatever the reason, the doorbell rang just fifteen minutes later, and within seconds Finn was escorting a middle-aged man into her bedroom. Kelly, who'd been lying by the side of the bed, leapt to her feet and gave a growl.

'Petra,' Finn said, 'this is Dr. Lewis. Kelly — ' He looked down at the dog. ' — come with me.' And both man and dog left the room.

Dr Lewis stood and regarded her for a long moment and then said, 'Finn tells me you've been very sick.'

A few minutes and several questions later, he confidently diagnosed a virus of some sort. 'There are all manner of things going around. So I suggest that you take plenty of fluids and try not to eat for twenty-four hours.'

'That won't be a problem,' she told him. The mere thought of food was sufficient to make her feel sick.

'No point giving you an antibiotic. It wouldn't do a bit of good.'

There was a knock on the door at that point.

'Come in, Finn,' the doctor called. 'We're finished.'

Finn's gaze went straight to Petra as he walked in.

'Some sort of stomach bug,' the doctor told him. 'Plenty of it around. I've told Ms Matthews to have plenty of liquids, preferably water, and no food for twenty-four hours.' He frowned then. 'She shouldn't really be alone. Is there anyone . . . ?'

'No need to call anyone else. I can stay. Thank you, Jim, for coming so speedily. It's much appreciated.'

He led the doctor from the room, glancing over his shoulder at Petra as he did so. 'I'll be back in a bit.'

'There's no need. I'll be okay.'

'I'll see Jim out.'

He was back almost at once. 'Is there anything you need?'

'Yes, one thing. Could you ring Debs at the gallery and tell her I won't be at the class tonight?' She couldn't imagine what Debs would make of Finn ringing her. The image that presented itself to her had her smiling weakly. She could imagine the sort of inquisition he'd be subjected to.

'Yes, of course.'

'Her number's in my pop-up by the phone.'

'I'll find it. Now stop worrying and try to sleep.'

The doorbell chimed again. 'That'll be Mother,' he told her. 'Are you up for a brief visit?' He raised a quizzical eyebrow.

'Of course.' How could she say no, after Elizabeth's extreme kindness?

He again went downstairs and sure enough, she heard Elizabeth's voice right before the sound of footsteps coming up the stairs.

Elizabeth crept into the room. 'Oh, my dear, how are you? I've brought you some chicken broth. My mother swore by it. And I always keep some in.' Her concern was only too evident as she scrutinised Petra's pale face.

Finn followed her in. 'Mother, that's for colds and flu. It won't do anything for sickness. In fact, it will probably exacerbate it.'

'Oh, okay. Well, keep it in the fridge for when Petra feels like eating again.'

'Thank you, Elizabeth. I'm so sorry for all this bother. You've been so kind — both of you.' She glanced sideways at Finn.

'It was no trouble, my dear. You looked so ill. And Finn doesn't mind, do you, Finn?' She beamed at her son and then at Petra. 'Now, if Finn's staying, can I make up a bed for him? I don't want you getting up, and — '

'The guestroom next to this room is already made up. I keep it that way, just in case . . . ' Her words petered out as she asked herself, in case of what? Her parents didn't want to visit, that was more than evident. Finn and Elizabeth both looked questioningly at her. 'In case my parents come to visit unexpectedly.'

'Oh,' Elizabeth cried. 'Should we ring them? How remiss of us. Finn?'

Finn frowned as Petra hastened to say, 'Oh no, please, don't do that. My mother will go straight into panic mode.' It was the only excuse she could think of. She could hardly tell them the truth, that her parents had no desire to visit her; at least, not yet. Although, recalling her mother's words, hope sprang up again within her. But Finn was still frowning. Did he not believe her? Knowing how perceptive he could be, probably not. 'I'm sure I'll be up and about again tomorrow.'

'Well, dear, looking at you now, I wouldn't bank on that,' Elizabeth declared. 'You do still look very poorly. Are you sure I can't ring them?'

'I'm sure.'

Once they'd both left the room again — Elizabeth must have kept the taxi waiting outside, because she didn't hear Finn leave — Petra did manage to sleep. Kelly loyally remained at her side, only leaving her to eat or drink. She'd been aware of her door opening a couple of times and Finn gazing at her, but she'd kept her eyes firmly closed and he'd quietly left again. It was mid-afternoon before she fell into a deep, feverish sleep punctuated by yet more lurid dreams. Once again there were people shouting at her, heaving stones at her, crowding round the cottage, peering in the windows, banging on her door.

As a result, she tossed and turned, flinging the duvet off her burning body, moaning, crying, 'Leave me alone — please. Don't hurt me. It wasn't me, it wasn't me.'

'Petra, Petra, wake up. You're dreaming.'

She was aware of someone lifting her up, holding her, a mouth pressed to her sweat-dampened hair. She eventually forced her eyes open and lifted her head. She saw Finn staring at her, his face creased with anxiety as he held her close and stroked the strands of hair from her eyes. Kelly was there too, her soulful eyes fixed fearfully on her mistress. Why was Finn here? Had he come to accuse her too?

'It wasn't my fault,' she cried. 'I didn't know. I didn't. You must believe me.'

Finn stroked her forehead. 'What wasn't your fault, sweetheart? What didn't you know?' His voice was soft, tender. 'You're ill, Petra. You have a temperature. It's okay. Sssh,' he soothed as she began to sob — heartbroken, deep-throated cries that wouldn't be stilled. And all the while, she shook and trembled. Finn held her even closer. So close, she could feel his heart beating. 'It's okay. There's no need to be scared. I'm here. I won't let anyone hurt you. I promise. You have my word.'

14

When eventually Petra managed to stem the flood of tears, she remained, half sitting, half lying against Finn, wishing she could stay this way forever, in his arms, knowing she'd be safe just as he'd promised.

However, that couldn't be, not without telling him the full story. Reluctantly, she dragged herself away from him.

'What's troubling you so much, Petra?' he quietly asked. 'Who — or what — are you afraid of? What wasn't your fault? It wasn't just the result of the fever, was it? There's something wrong. Tell me. Maybe I can help?'

'No one can help,' she blurted. 'It's far too late for that.'

He continued to watch her, his gaze narrowed with speculation. 'Petra . . . '

The doorbell rang, and she heard his

muttered, 'Damn,' his tone now one of utter frustration.

Once he'd left the room, Petra lay back against the pillows, reliving the moments when he'd held her close, his lips against her hair, and she smiled to herself. It was beginning to look as if Elizabeth was right. He must genuinely care about her to be doing this. But would he still care if he knew who she really was? And would he believe in her self-proclaimed innocence?

The sound of voices in the hallway distracted her from these disturbing questions. One was clearly Finn's, the other a woman. It wasn't Elizabeth. Suddenly, the bedroom door opened and Debs stood there. Kelly gave a low growl which almost at once turned into a yelp of excited welcome.

'Petra, how are you? When Finn rang, I was worried. I had to come.' She didn't look worried, however, and her smile was a broad one as she whispered, 'How the hell have you managed this? To get the gorgeous Finn

Hog . . . ' She stopped talking just as Finn appeared behind her.

Petra prayed she'd been in time and Finn hadn't overheard her words. That hope was immediately dashed, however, when she spotted the gleam in his eye as he strode into the room bearing a fresh jug of water.

'I thought you might need this,' he explained.

'Th-thank you.' She didn't dare look at Debs to see what she was making of it all. She was sure she'd hear soon enough. And she was right.

Finn had barely left the room again before she was hissing, 'You jammy beggar. What wouldn't I give to have Finn Hogarth nursing me. What the hell happened?'

'I was taken ill at Greystones. Elizabeth phoned him to come and drive me back here. I didn't ask him to stay,' she went on. 'He insisted.'

'Yeah, well, he's crazy about you. Anyone with half an eye can see that.'

'He's taken pity on me, that's all.'

'Right.' Debs rolled her eyes. 'Tell that to the marines.'

Petra gave a low laugh. 'I would if I knew any.'

'Okay, so come on. What's been going on between you two? Because it's screamingly apparent something has. Why else would he be here nursing you?'

So Petra, keeping her voice low, told her about the two occasions Finn had taken her out.

'And what happened? Did he make mad, passionate love to you?'

'No, not really.'

'Liar. He did, didn't he?'

Petra shrugged. 'We kissed, that's all.'

'That's all?' Debs was practically shrieking now. 'That's all?'

'Sssh. He'll hear,' she hissed.

Debs did lower her voice at that, but Petra refused to say anything more on that particular subject. Instead, she went on, 'So how come you're here? Who's minding the gallery?'

'I closed, for personal reasons. Mind

you, I didn't realise quite how personal they'd be.' Debs lowered one eyelid in a provocative wink. 'Anyway, it's not long to closing time.'

Petra ignored her suggestive innuendo. 'I see.'

'Look, I'd better go. I need to prepare for this evening. I just wanted to see how you were for myself, and I have to say you don't look well, lovey. Is there anything I can get you? I could pop back after the class.'

'No, there's no need for that. Finn has everything in hand.'

'I'll bet he has, especially you.' And she cocked an eyebrow.

Petra rolled her eyes. 'Goodbye, Debs,' she firmly said. 'Hopefully I'll see you next week. Um — before you go, there is something. You couldn't bring me up my laptop, could you? I need to check my emails. It's in the sitting room, on the coffee table.'

'Course I will.' And she hurried from the room and down the stairs. Petra heard Finn's voice, although she couldn't hear what he was saying, and then Debs reappeared, laptop in hand. 'He tried to stop me bringing this up,' she whispered. 'He says you shouldn't be worrying about emails. You're too sick. I ignored him, naturally. So here you are. Actually, though, he's right. Don't go overdoing things, and I'll see you soon.'

'Thanks, Debs. I'll be up and about again by tomorrow, hopefully.'

'I doubt that, looking at you now. But see you.' And with a little wave, she was gone.

★   ★   ★

Quickly, and before Finn could put in an appearance, Petra logged onto her webmail. She had two new emails in her inbox. They'd come in within the last half hour. They were both from Nemesis.

With a heartbeat that felt powerful enough to explode from her chest, she clicked onto the first: YOU HAVEN'T

PAID THE MONEY BACK, SO IT WON'T BE LONG NOW. I'M WATCHING YOU. WAITING.

The second said, BELIEVE WHAT I SAY. I'LL BE COMING FOR YOU. SOON.

She sank back against the pillows, panic flooding her, her gaze glued to the words on her screen. Whoever this was, they were determined to punish her; to exact their notion of retribution.

Which led her on to another even more important question. Could whoever this was really be preparing to harm her? Or was it all an empty threat designed to simply inflict terror on her? She re-read both emails. The first one was bad enough. 'I'm watching you. Waiting.' How could this person be watching her? Standing somewhere outside the cottage; following her everywhere she went? She'd have noticed, wouldn't she? Unless — there was more than one person? Maybe they were out there now? However, it was the second one that proved the most

304

disturbing. 'I'll be coming for you. Soon.' How soon? And what would they do when they came?

Shaking with fear now, she climbed from bed and crept to the window. It looked directly out onto the road. She stared up and down it as far as she could see. There was no one there. So if she were being watched, where were they watching her from? Maybe they were further away than she thought, and using binoculars.

She shivered and headed back towards the bed. Before she got there, though, Finn walked in. 'You could have knocked,' she blurted. The T-shirt she was wearing only barely covered the essential bits of her. Her legs were bare all the way up to her bottom, and even that wasn't fully covered. She tugged hard at the hem, trying to pull it further down. She heard the stitching tear.

'For heaven's sake.' His expression now was a grim one. 'I have seen a woman's legs before, you know. And I assumed you'd be lying in bed — where you should be — under the duvet.'

'You should never assume,' she snapped back, only to instantly regret her sharpness. He didn't deserve that. 'I-I'm sorry.'

He ignored the apology, although she noted a warmer gleam to his eye. 'Perhaps you'd like to tell me what the hell you're doing out of bed?'

She tried to hurry back to it, but instead lost her already precarious balance. She staggered and would have fallen if Finn hadn't leapt towards her, catching her just in time. It was at that point that she realised her laptop was still open, the final email there on the screen. Finn would be bound to see it.

She tugged free of his hold. 'I-I can manage.'

He released her instantly, holding both hands defensively in the air and away from her. 'Fine. If you say so.'

She climbed onto the bed, closing the laptop as she did so.

His look then was a scornful one. 'Oh, don't worry. I wasn't about to read whatever was on there.'

'S-sorry,' she said again.

'Don't be. Your private mail is just that, private.' But his eyes had narrowed as he stood over her, hands on his hips. 'Boyfriend, is it?'

'I don't have a boyfriend — as you well know.'

He shrugged, as if it mattered not a jot to him whether she did or not. 'Well, I know you said you weren't interested in getting involved with anyone, but I'm sure you must have admirers.'

'No.'

'Really? Not even one?'

'No, not even one.'

'You astonish me. A woman as lovely as you.'

Yeah, right. If she had the strength, she'd laugh at that. Because she must look anything but alluring at the moment. Hang on, was he being sarcastic; mocking her, even? She slanted an accusing gaze at him. He didn't look as if he were taking the mickey. In fact, there was a very disturbing look to him now; a smouldering look. Surely he couldn't fancy her looking as she did? And when all he said was, 'How are you feeling? Hungry?' she decided she'd imagined it.

'No, not at all. I wouldn't say no to a cup of tea, though. No milk. And . . .' She paused; she didn't want to be too demanding. 'Kelly probably needs to go out. Could you let her into the garden?'

'Sure. I'll take her for a walk if you like — just a short one. Are you okay with that?'

'Of course. Thank you, Finn. You're being so . . . ' She didn't quite know how to phrase it. *Kind* sounded so mediocre.

He gave a crooked grin. 'I know — so kind. It's very easy to be kind to you, Petra. That's no problem. It's getting closer to you that's the real problem.' And with that, he left the room.

Petra lay back down, pondering his final words. At least her stomach felt more settled, so that was an improvement. But what was she going to do about these anonymous emails? Maybe she should answer them?

The door opened and Finn walked back in, holding a large mug of tea.

'Thank you,' she meekly said.

He didn't respond to that other than to say, 'Time for a walk, Kelly.'

Kelly leapt to her feet and headed for the open door, but not before looking back at Petra, her quizzical gaze asking, 'Will you be all right?'

'Go on,' Petra murmured. 'I'll be fine.'

Once she heard the front door open and then close once more, she sat up and opened her laptop. She had made a decision. She was not going to be made a victim; not again. She refused to simply sit back and allow someone to intimidate and scare her. Not this time. This time, she'd fight back.

She opened the last email that had arrived, hit REPLY, and began to type.

'I don't know who you are or why

you're doing this to me, but if you don't stop I'll inform the police. I'm sure they'll have ways of tracing you. I've done nothing to you and I had nothing to do with what my husband did. He's paid the ultimate price with his life and that's an end to it. Now, LEAVE ME ALONE. She hit SEND and waited.

It wasn't until she'd drunk her tea that a new email pinged into her inbox. She opened it. It wasn't written in capital letters this time. That made it seem less menacing, although, in reality it wasn't. The words were just as threatening.

'I'm someone who wants to see justice done. You're the same as your greedy husband because you must have known what he was doing. And you must have shared his ill-gotten gains. With your big house, your fast cars, your expensive holidays, your designer clothes. That makes you just as guilty. You weren't clever enough. I recognised you despite your pathetic attempt at a disguise. And telling the police won't help you. It'll only mean your identity being made public. I'll still get to you. So, I'm warning you. Watch your back. It's payback time on behalf of all the innocent people you robbed. It won't be long now. Nemesis, the deliverer of justice.'

She read the words over and over. There could be no mistake. Someone in this town intended her harm. She slumped back onto her pillows. What the hell was she to do? There seemed no way out for her. If she stayed here, she would be in danger. If she told the police what was happening and her identity was made known — which it almost certainly would be, as Nemesis pointed out — she'd have to leave Poltreath anyway. So she might as well go before all that happened.

A small sob forced its way up her throat just as she heard the front door opening and the sounds of Kelly and Finn returning. Kelly instantly raced up the stairs to her, Finn followed more slowly. She closed her laptop just as

Finn strode into the room. His gaze moved instantly to her. 'What's wrong? Has something happened?' His expression had sharpened.

Good grief. What sort of power did this man have? The sort that could see straight through her, read her every thought?

'No. I'm just tired, that's all.'

'Have you been sick again?'

She shook her head. 'Do you know, I'm feeling a bit better. I think I'd like to come downstairs for a while. Watch a bit of TV. It's rather boring up here.'

'You just said you were tired. Which is it? Tired or better?'

'Better — but a little tired still, as well. Good grief, it's like being on trial.'

'Well, you do still look very pale, but if you're sure, it's your decision.'

'Yes, it is.' She pushed the duvet to one side. 'Could you pass me my dressing gown on the back of the door?'

Still looking doubtful, he handed it to her. Without as much as a glance Finn's way, she slipped the gown on. The truth was she was still feeling as weak as hell, but she was determined to get up. She glanced down over herself as she tied the belt around her waist. The gown wasn't all that clean, but it would have to do. She slanted a glance at him. She'd love to know what he was thinking. That she was a grubby slut probably. One who didn't bother laundering her clothes.

'Let me give you a hand.'

If he had been thinking such thoughts, he gave no sign of it.

He slipped an arm around her waist and clasped her one hand in his. Together, they left the room and began to descend the stairs, Kelly bringing up the rear. But it soon became more than evident that she wasn't as well as she'd insisted, and they were only halfway down the stairs when the nausea arose again.

'Oh no,' she gasped. 'I need to get back to the bathroom — quickly.'

Finn didn't hesitate. He hoisted her into his arms and, by some feat of

313

superhuman agility, managed to get her there in time. She crouched over the toilet bowl, where, with Finn still holding her and Kelly whining just behind her, she was sick yet again.

Once she was done, and it hadn't been the volume or as violent as it had been previously, she was glad to say, he lifted her into his arms again and transported her to the bedroom and her bed.

'Sorry, sorry,' she wept, 'I'm so sorry.'

'Will you stop saying you're sorry,' he curtly told her. 'There's absolutely no need. But,' he added as he examined her closely, 'are you sure it's just the stomach bug now that's making you ill? You were looking better — well, a bit more colour, at any rate — before Kelly and I went out. What happened in that time? Because something did. I'd put money on it.'

'It's nothing, really.' If only she could confide in him. Seek his advice as to what she should do. Because she sure as hell didn't know. But if she confessed the truth, then what? He'd hate her, just as her tormentor did.

Tears welled and stung her eyes. She grabbed the glass of water and drank half of it. Her mouth was feeling like the pits. Oh no. Did her breath smell? Was she stinking of BO as well as vomit? She huddled down beneath the duvet, trying to cover as much of herself as she could.

Finn perched on the side of the bed and took hold of the hand nearest to him that was poking out from beneath the duvet. It was the only part of her, besides her head, that was visible.

'You can tell me, whatever it is. There's not much that can shock me anymore.' He paused, his gaze a searching one. 'Petra, I care about you; really care.' Something kindled in his eyes. Desire? No, it couldn't be. No man in his right mind would desire her the way she looked now.

'Finn, I-I told you. I can't become involved, not with you, not with anyone. There are things you don't know. Things I can't — talk about.'

'What things? You haven't murdered someone, have you?' He spoke lightly, but his expression was a serious one.

She stared at him, shocked that he could even think such a thing, let alone voice it. 'No, of course I haven't. But . . . ' She stopped right there. She'd almost told him then. She was way too vulnerable at the moment. She had to get him out of her room, before she weakened and actually told him the truth.

'But?'

'But nothing. Believe me, you don't want to be involved with me.' Again, she stopped talking. 'Look, if you don't mind, I'd like to sleep.'

'Fine.' But he stayed where he was, still watching her.

Petra closed her eyes against that searching gaze before, to her relief, she heard the bed creak as he got up. Still, she kept her eyes tightly closed.

'Okay. If that's what you want.' Despite the ordinariness of the words, she suspected he was miffed. 'Try to sleep, then. Come on, Kelly. We're not wanted here, so let's go downstairs.'

But Kelly obviously didn't want to do that, because the only sound Petra heard was that of Finn leaving the room — alone.

15

Petra sat up and opened her laptop again, leaving it open before closing her eyes in what she suspected would be a vain attempt to sleep. But she must have managed it, because the room was in darkness when a ping alerted her to the fact that another email had arrived. It was from Nemesis. Just two words. 'Look outside.'

Quietly, so as not to alert Finn to the fact that she was awake, she climbed out of bed. She was alone. Kelly must have quietly left the room while she slept and gone downstairs, presumably in the hope that Finn would take her for one last walk. Petra didn't turn on a light. She crept to the window and, pulling a curtain to one side, peered out. A solitary figure stood in the patch of front garden. A figure dressed all in black: black trousers and a black hoodie. If she hadn't known someone was there, she didn't think she'd have spotted them, because they merged perfectly into the night-time darkness. There wasn't even a moon to illuminate things.

As she stared down, the figure lifted an arm and waved, before hurling something up at her window. Petra instinctively stepped back as what looked like a large stone fractured the glass, sending slivers flying into the room like miniature arrows, before it dropped again to the ground beneath her window. The shock of it sent Petra reeling backwards and before she could do anything to save herself, she fell, banging her head hard on the floor.

Kelly began to bark and she heard Finn say, 'What the hell was that? It sounded . . . ' She couldn't hear what else he said, and the next thing she heard was Finn mounting the stairs — at a run by the sound of it. He erupted into her room, turned on the overhead light, and saw her, sprawled

319

flat amongst the fragments of glass. He strode straight to her and carefully lifted her up. 'What the hell's happened? Are you hurt?'

He carried her to the bed and sat her down upon it before asking, 'Are you cut anywhere?' He glanced round the room again, in particular at the glass scattered on the floor.

'I don't think so,' Petra whispered. 'There was someone outside. They threw a stone up.'

He strode to the window and looked out. 'Nobody there now.' He swung to look at Petra. 'Could you see who it was?'

'No.'

He walked back to her and plumped himself down onto the bed by the side of her. 'Are you sure you're okay?'

She lifted a hand to the back of her head and gingerly explored amongst the tousled strands of hair. 'I-I think so. There was someone out there — definitely. When they threw the stone, I-I was startled and stepped back too quickly. I lost my balance.'

'Do I need to call Jim? Let me have a look,' he said, before gently examining the back of her head and pronouncing, 'You'll live. The skin's not broken. You'll probably have a bruise, though — and a headache.' He gently laid her down before regarding her once more. 'You said you saw someone, but couldn't see who it was.'

'That's right. It's very dark out there — no streetlights. And he-he was dressed all in black with a hoodie partially hiding his face. Whoever it was just stood there looking up at me, waving.' Her words tailed off in a small sob. 'I just saw him throw something. It dropped back to the ground. It would have hit me if-if it had actually smashed through the window.' Her voice finally broke.

And just like before, Finn pulled her close to him, cradling her against his chest as if she were a child, once again making Petra feel as if nothing could hurt her. 'I don't want to nag, but this is important. Was it an adult, or a young person?'

'Whoever it was didn't look very big, so I suppose it could have been a young person — or even a woman.' Oh my God. Could it have been Isobel? She wasn't sufficiently convinced of that, though, to name names, so instead she said, 'I'm sorry. It was only a moment's glimpse, then the stone came flying at me.'

'So they saw you standing in the window and threw the stone at you.' He was frowning, clearly disturbed by what had happened. 'My car is parked outside. They must have known someone was with you.'

'Yes, but they still did it.'

'How did you know someone was out there? Did they call you?'

She shook her head. 'No. They emailed me. Told me to look outside. To find out where I was in the house, I suppose, and if I was alone.'

He pulled his mobile phone from his shirt pocket, his narrowed glance still upon her.

'What are you doing?'

322

'Calling the police, of course.'

'No,' she cried. 'Please — don't do that.'

'Why the hell not?' He stared at her. 'Are you sure you don't know who it was?'

'Yes, I'm sure, but I don't want a fuss — please. It was most likely local lads.'

'Why would they email you first? He frowned. 'Have you had other emails?'

She nodded her head.

He didn't speak straight away. Then: 'They were what you didn't want me to see?'

She nodded again.

'S-o . . . ' His gaze narrowed at her. She could sense him mentally collating the facts. 'First of all, your tyres were slashed, then emails, now this. How many emails?'

She decided to come clean with him. 'Four before this last one, and there were two anonymous letters as well. They came first.'

'Christ. So you're clearly a target for someone. Why? What reason could they possibly have to do this to you?'

Petra pulled free of his embrace and lay back against her pillows, closing her eyes, protecting herself from his penetrating gaze. She couldn't fight him anymore. She was too tired.

'I don't know,' she whispered. She couldn't tell him the truth.

But he pulled her back up, holding her by the shoulders and shaking her gently, thereby persuading her to look at him. 'Are you sure about that? Talk to me, Petra. Tell me what's happening. Maybe I can help.'

'I don't think you can. No one can help me. Even my family can't help me.' She looked away from him. 'No one believes me when I say — when I say . . .'

He placed his one hand under her chin, this time compelling her to look at him. 'What? Say what? You've obviously been dreaming about it. For God's sake, Petra, tell me. You won't shock me, if that's what you're worried about. I've heard most things by now.'

'Not this,' she muttered. 'You won't have had anyone tell you this before. Believe me.'

'So tell me. I can't bear to see you so-so devastated.'

She took a deep breath, readying herself for his contempt. 'Petra is my middle name. My real Christian name is Alicia, and-and my surname isn't Matthews, it's . . . ' She drew a shaky breath. 'It's Cornell.'

Finn's eyebrows rose. 'Cornell? Why do I know that name?'

My-my husband, Grant Cornell, was being investigated for — for . . . '

Finn's expression had darkened. 'Go on.' His grip tightened fractionally on her shoulders, as if he were trying to support her in some way.

Reassured as well as comforted by that, she managed to continue. 'For pension fraud; his employees' pensions. He-he didn't pay the firm's contributions.'

Finn didn't speak for a long, long moment. Petra could actually feel his shock, his disgust. She tried to pull away. He tightened his grip.

'I remember. I remember the story — he killed himself; there were pictures of you both — all over the front pages.' He held her away from him then, studying her intently for a long, long moment. 'I can see it now I know. Yet, there's something not right . . . ' He scrutinised her from beneath lowered lids. She was about to tell him it was probably the colour of her eyes and hair, when he pulled her back into his arms. 'As I understood it, it was finally concluded you had nothing to do with his fraudulent activities.'

'No, of course I didn't. I had no idea what he was doing, but no one would believe me. Everyone believed I must have known — even my family. And how could I not have known? I should have known,' she wailed. 'He'd been spending so much money. I should have questioned him more about where it was all coming from, not-not just accepted what he told me.'

'So why didn't you?' Finn quietly asked.

'I tried, when his spending seemed out of control, but he-he looked as if he was about to hit me, so I stopped. I believed him when he said the businesses were making huge sums of money. I actually believed him. I'm so stupid . . .'

Tears seeped from her eyes. She dashed them away. 'Once it became known what he'd done, after he'd died — my home was targeted, attacked, windows smashed, paint smeared over doors. My car tyres were let down. It went on and on. I'd think it was over and it would start again. I couldn't really blame people. Their pensions, their jobs, they stood to lose so much.' Her tears overflowed now, uncontrollably, as she struggled to speak. 'My-my parents refused to believe I didn't know about it. They won't visit me. My brother hasn't spoken to me since. After a while, I decided I couldn't take any more and-and I came here. I dyed my hair from blonde to brown, used coloured contact lenses to change my eyes . . . ' Her weeping slowed. Again, she dashed the tears from her face.

Finn bent his head, the better to study her.

'I've slept in them, I'm afraid. I thought you'd notice the sudden change if I took them out.'

'What colour are your eyes, normally?'

'Blue.'

'Ri-ight. Well, you'd better remove them now, hadn't you?'

She nodded and quickly did so, placing them in their container in the drawer at the side of her bed.

'My God, it does change your appearance, doesn't it?'

'Yes, but not sufficiently, obviously. Someone's recognised me. I even lost weight, not deliberately; it just happened. But — someone knows who I am, and I'm being attacked again, this time with anonymous letters and emails. If-if it all gets out, no one will believe me, just like before.'

Finn wrapped her in his arms, pressing his mouth into her hair. 'I believe you.'

She raised her head and stared at him, her eyes wide and luminous. 'Do you? Honestly?'

'Yes. Tell me what the emails said?'

'That they're coming after me. That someone has to pay. Justice has to be done. It's someone calling themselves Nemesis.'

'Show me,' he grimly said.

She swung her laptop round to face him and watched as his features hardened and darkened, as his top lip curled with contempt, but not for her, for the writer of these awful words. She even showed him her response to Nemesis.

'The police will soon trace these back to the sender.'

'No, please.' This was exactly what she'd been terrified of. Because even if her persecutor didn't make Grant's crime public, once the police knew, it would almost certainly be leaked anyway. And that meant one thing only. She'd lose everything all over again. 'I'll lose my business, like before, just as I'm getting started. Nobody wants the wife of a thief in their homes, I quickly found that out. And your parents — what would they say?'

'They'd believe you, just as I have. Nobody in their right mind would believe you were connected to such things. And as for these emails, they're clearly from a deeply disturbed individual, not to say deranged.'

'Please, I beg you, don't involve the police. It's all bound to come out. I wouldn't be able to bear that.'

'But you're not on your own now, and you never will be.'

What did that mean? That he wanted to be with her? Stay with her?

'But this latest incident has changed things. Someone has tried to hurt you physically. Who knows what else they'll try?'

He was echoing her fears. 'I've got

Kelly. She's a good guard dog.'

'That's as may be, but even she can't protect you if someone genuinely means you harm.'

'Please don't call the police. Let's wait and see what happens. I'm sure it's empty threats, intended to frighten me. When I don't react.'

'But you have reacted. You've replied to the emails.'

'I won't do that again. It didn't help.'

He eyed her, his scepticism plain to see. 'Okay, I'll do nothing for now, but I'm going to be keeping a very close eye on you.' He fell silent, his expression a reflective one. 'I love you, you know. And I'm hoping you might feel the same way about me?' He didn't seem sure about that, however. He lifted an eyebrow at her, clearly hoping for an answer. 'I know you said you didn't want to get involved, and belatedly I understand why. But I know the truth now, so . . .'

'I do,' she blurted. 'I mean, I do feel the same way. I tried not to, because I couldn't be honest about who I was. It was so hard, and frankly, it was a losing battle right from the start.' She managed a shaky smile.

The look he gave her then told her more plainly than words could have how he felt about her admission. 'Oh, my darling,' he breathed, dragging her close once more. He buried his face in her hair a second time, then he kissed her eyelids, her cheeks.

'I need a shower, and to clean my teeth,' she weakly protested.

'No, you're not strong enough. Maybe in the morning. For now, lie down and try to sleep. Forget what's happened. I'm here. Just let anyone try anything else and they'll have more to deal with than they expected. A whole lot more.'

She smiled drowsily up at him, loving the way his eyes softened and gleamed, as he bent his head and kissed her, so very gently, and so very lovingly.

16

Feeling loved and cherished for the first time in a long while, Petra slept, dreamlessly and deeply. So deeply, she didn't hear Finn creeping back into the bedroom to clear up the broken glass and cover the hole in the window pane by taping a piece of cardboard over it.

So it was that, come morning, Petra awoke not only to the sun streaming through the curtains, but also to the unfamiliar feeling of hope. It was as if an enormous weight had been lifted from her just by telling Finn what had been happening, telling him the truth, at last. And he'd believed in her innocence. So if he did, maybe — just maybe — others would too, if she gave them the opportunity.

She was far too happy to waste time lying in bed. She glanced at the clock on the bedside table and saw that it was after nine. Kelly had already left her to go in search of Finn, breakfast, and possibly a walk. Petra sprang up, relieved to discover all trace of the virus she'd been suffering from miraculously gone. She headed for the bathroom and the longed-for shower and was soon softly singing to herself as she soaped her body and shampooed her hair. She slipped on her dressing gown, not bothering to fasten the belt around her, leaving the two sides flapping freely around her. It was as she headed for her bedroom that she came face to face with Finn, a broadly grinning Finn as he took in the sight of the curves so carelessly left on display. Petra felt her face flame as she hastily tugged the two sides together. Finn, of course, was fully clothed.

'You sound happy. I take it you feel better this morning?'

'I feel like a different woman,' she shyly told him.

He slid his arms inside her dressing

gown, pulling her closely to him, gently caressing her, running his hands over her curves, stoking up her desire until it was threatening to consume her. 'Mmm, you feel the same to me,' he huskily murmured, his expression one of barely contained lust. He bent his head and kissed her before removing his hands from her and gently slapping her bottom, as he murmured, 'Off you go and get dressed. I only have so much willpower and I can feel that slipping away as I speak. I've prepared you some breakfast. I was intending to bring it up to you, but I can see that you're almost ready to come downstairs.'

'I'll be five minutes,' she told him. 'Can you keep it warm?' And she fluttered her eyelids suggestively at him.

He gave a shout of laughter. 'I most certainly can. Actually,' he murmured, 'I've been keeping it warm for a while now.'

It was as she headed for her bedroom that her conscience got the better of her and she said, 'Look — I'm feeling fine now, so please don't feel you have to stay with me. You must have some business to attend to?'

'Well, there are a couple of things,' he told her, albeit doubtfully, 'but I'll gladly stay.'

'I'm sure you would, but there's really no need. Um — do you think your mother will mind if I don't get back to the work until Monday? I feel as if I need a couple more days to make sure I'm really okay.'

'Of course she won't. I'll call in and tell her. She'll probably ring you. She's the closest thing I know to a mother hen when there's anything wrong with the people she loves. You might even have her here, watching over you. Which might not be a bad thing under the circumstances.'

'Oh no, really. There's no need. I've been enough of a bother as it is. And . . . ' She shyly eyed him. ' . . . I don't think she loves me.'

'Believe me, Petra, she does. She fell

for you almost as fast as I did. And you are not a bother. In fact,' he added, concern dragging his brow down, 'I think I will stay. The business will wait till Monday.'

'No,' she insisted, 'I'll be fine. No one's going to do anything to me in broad daylight. Please, Finn. I'll feel bad if you stay. And let's not forget I've got Kelly.

'Hmmm. I'm not sure how much help she'd be — but okay, if you're sure.'

'I am. But you won't tell your parents yet, will you? About Grant? I'd rather tell them myself.'

'Of course, I won't. It's your call. Now, get dressed and come down for breakfast.' He swivelled, preparing to descend the stairs, but then stopped and turned back to her. 'Uh — what shall I call you now?'

'Petra,' she told him. 'I prefer it to Alicia.'

'Okay, Petra you will remain.'

Kelly, of course, was overjoyed to see

her up and about. She danced around Petra's legs, barking, whining, wriggling, tail swinging like a metronome, so intense was her rapture. Once breakfast was over, Finn told her, 'I'll be back by five thirty this afternoon. I'm not leaving you alone overnight.' He narrowed his eyes at her as he went on, 'And I mean that literally. Your bed looks plenty big enough for two.' He finished with a deliberately sensuous look.

'Mmm, promises, promises.' And she also half closed her eyes, peeking up at him through lowered lashes.

'Oh, it's a promise all right. In fact,' he added, glancing at his wrist watch, 'I do have a bit of time now.' Sheer lust glittered at her once again.

Somehow, she resisted the offer and waved him off. 'Off you go. I've got things to do as well.'

So he contented himself with a kiss, long and passionate, parting her lips to slide his tongue inside. So aroused was she, she almost pleaded for him to stay.

Somehow, though, she restrained herself.

He eventually released her. 'I'll contact a glazier I know and get him to come ASAP and repair that broken window.'

'Thank you.' And with that, he was gone.

It wasn't till then that she remembered her van was still at Greystones. Not that it mattered. She had her car in the garage. Anyway, if she went anywhere, she'd walk. The fresh air would do her good; complete her recovery, in fact. But her first task, after the glazier had been, would be to take Kelly out. She'd walk her into town. But firstly, she'd ring Elizabeth. She'd been so kind, kinder than her own mother had been as a matter of fact. Although she supposed that wasn't really fair. Elizabeth, unlike her mother, didn't know the truth about her circumstances.

Once the window had been replaced, she set off for her walk. She'd call in on

Debs, she decided; let her see that she was fully recovered and perhaps have a coffee with her. She suspected she'd have to answer a multitude of questions about Finn, but strangely, she wouldn't mind. If anything, she was looking forward to talking about him. She smiled to herself. Now that she knew he loved her, nothing else mattered.

But apart from the opportunity to talk about Finn, she wanted to buy ingredients for a dinner for two. He, just like his mother, had been so kind, so thoughtful, so patient, and she wanted to repay him. Although she suspected that making love with him would be repayment enough. She smiled to herself, heady anticipation shafting through her

Debs greeted her with a combination of pleasure and surprise that she had so swiftly recovered and, exactly as Petra had expected, a zillion questions about what was happening between her and Finn.

She began with, 'Well, I can see

you're better. Is that down to the nursing abilities of the gorgeous Finn, or something more — um, intimate?' She eyed Petra, a wicked glint to her eyes before continuing with, 'He did stay the night with you?'

'He did, but there was nothing like you're suggesting. It was perfectly proper. He stayed in the guest room and I remained in my own.'

'How disappointing.' Debs pouted. 'Anyway, I'm pretty sure he'll make up for that tonight. Because to my mind any man who stays and nurses a sick woman must have pretty serious intentions towards her.'

'Well . . . ' Petra gave a tiny smile. ' . . . you might be right.'

'Oh dear. That won't please a certain gentleman.'

Petra lifted an enquiring eyebrow.

'Marcus. He looked pretty let down when you didn't show last evening. I think he's got his sights on you as well.'

'No, he knows that's a no go. I made it very clear.' She recalled his expression when she'd told him that. He'd been furious; outraged, in fact. So outraged that if the assailant the evening before had been taller, bigger, she would have given serious consideration to him being the guilty party. As it was, he looked to be out of the running.

'So,' Debs said, 'do you want a coffee? I've just made a pot.'

★ ★ ★

It was as they drunk their coffee that Petra asked if Debs had heard how Isabel's husband, Tom, was.

'Not well, as far as I know. He's still in hospital. Not surprisingly, Isobel didn't turn up last night for painting. But then, she's probably not in the mood for that. However, I did hear that Sally and Tara are thinking of finding their own place to give Isobel and Tom — when he finally returns home, *if* he returns home — a bit of space. Although how they'll manage that I don't know. The last I heard, Sally was completely broke.'

With her coffee drunk and the shopping done, Petra said goodbye and set off for the cottage. She'd bought a couple of fillet steaks, salad, and baby new potatoes, and for starters she'd managed to get some smoked mackerel. She planned to make a mousse. For dessert she'd bought fresh raspberries, strawberries and blueberries, with a summer pudding in mind. She made one last purchase, a large tub of Cornish cream, before heading home. She sighed with happiness as she walked back. She'd never felt so contented, so loved, and so in love.

As soon as she arrived home, she began her preparations for that evening, which meant that by the time four o'clock came round she was exhausted. She made a pot of tea and took a cup into the sitting room. She'd tidied and polished until everything gleamed. She'd bought flowers, and they were attractively arranged in a vase on the window sill. The kitchen had received the same comprehensive treatment, but now she wondered if she'd overdone things, because she felt utterly weary and she still had to cook the meal she'd prepared earlier.

Nevertheless, once she'd drunk her tea, she took Kelly out again before returning to relax once more on the settee. She didn't want to be ill this evening; it would spoil everything. She checked the time. It was almost five o'clock. Only another half an hour and Finn would be here. A thrill of anticipation pierced her. She sensed her life was about to change forever.

She planned for them to eat at seven thirty. It would allow time to relax with a drink. She'd bought a couple of bottles of wine, and had even splurged on a bottle of Prosecco; she couldn't afford champagne. It was a poor substitute, but she didn't think Finn would mind.

She was lying on the settee, eyes closed, trying to snatch five minutes' sleep, when the doorbell rang. Once again, she glanced at the clock. It was only five fifteen. Finn was early. Her spirits lifted and her heart throbbed. Why was he ringing the bell? She'd given him a key. She smiled tenderly to herself. Maybe he didn't want to presume too much, not yet. She'd never misjudged anyone the way she'd misjudged Finn.

She got to her feet and walked into the hallway, checking her appearance in the wall mirror as she went. Seeing that the colour was back in her cheeks, she hurried to the door, flinging it open, and saying, 'Why didn't you use your — '

She stopped talking as she stared at the person standing on the step. It was the last person she'd expected to see.

'Why, Tara — what a surprise. Is everything okay? Your grandmother — '

'It's all fine. Well . . . ' She shrugged. ' . . . except for Granddad. He's still not good. Can I come in?' she unexpectedly asked. 'I want to talk to you about something.' She was clutching a bag to her chest; cradling it, in fact.

Kelly, who was standing just behind Petra, gave a low growl.

'It's okay, Kelly. It's Tara. Remember Tara?' She looked back at the girl. Tara was looking excited; overstrung, even. Her eyes blazed feverishly against the pallor of her skin. She looked ill. As ill as Petra had been. 'Are you okay? Do you need to sit down? Have a drink of water?' Petra closed the door behind the girl and led her into the sitting room. 'Please — have a seat. Tell me whatever it is that's worrying you and then I'll drive you home. You look as if you should be in bed.' She indicated one of the two armchairs.

But Tara only glanced at it before saying, 'No, I'll stand.'

Petra eyed her. There was still a strange look to her. 'Are you sure? You don't look yourself.'

'I'm fine.' She fell silent then, staring at Petra. 'I know who you are,' she then said in a low voice. 'I looked on my gran's laptop.'

Petra froze. 'Wh-what do you mean?'

'What I've just said. Are you deaf? I-know-who-you-are.' She spoke as if addressing an idiot. 'You're Alicia Cornell. Gran found you online. She was so quick to close the laptop when I walked into the room, I knew something was up. So I waited till she went into the kitchen and then I had a look. I found what she'd been looking at. Photos of you and your husband. I knew she'd been suspicious about you for a while, but it was Granddad turning up and obviously so ill — all the fault of you and your thieving husband — that must have triggered a memory of some sort.

'Anyway, something made her start searching online. I'd heard her talking to a friend, saying you wouldn't tell anyone about yourself, not even where you'd come from. She said you must have something to hide. No one is naturally that secretive. But apart from that, she was sure she'd seen you somewhere before. She went back through newspaper archives and found you. It was all there, the full story, photographs, the lot. She must have been absolutely furious, although she never said a word to me. She obviously blames you and your husband for Granddad's breakdown. The only difference between her and me is, I decided to do something about it. Make you suffer as we've suffered. Between the two of you, you've destroyed my granddad. He'll probably be in a mental hospital for months, if not years.'

Her mouth twisted in a sneer then as her gaze raked Petra. 'And if you tried to disguise yourself, you didn't do a very good job. Why didn't you just die, like he did? If you'd been in the car with him, you would have. And the world would have been a better place.' She looked almost demented by this time. Her skin was the colour of skimmed milk; even her lips were bloodless. Her eyes still blazed with hatred.

'So,' Petra struggled to speak, to

somehow contain her growing fear, 'was it you sending me the letters, the emails? Did you also slash the car tyres and heave the stone last night? Are you Nemesis?'

'Yeah. Great name, eh? Most appropriate, I thought. We've been doing Greek mythology at school. That's what gave me the idea.' The girl's mouth twisted into something that was more of a grimace than a smile. 'It was all me. Everything. The first letter I pushed through your door really early in the morning. I sneaked out while Gran and Mum were watching telly to leave the second. I was a bit nervous in case you were in and heard me, but you weren't. When I did your tyres, you weren't even out of bed. In fact, it was only just light. I had to set my alarm for that. Nobody heard a thing. It was much easier to send the emails. No chance of being seen either. I don't know why I didn't think of that in the first place. Then I sneaked out last night to throw the stone. Once Gran and Mum have got the telly on, they don't hear a thing. They had no idea what I was getting up to. It did put me off, seeing someone else's car outside, but then you came to the bedroom window — alone — so I just threw it. Did it scare you? Did the emails? They should have done. I meant every word.' She sounded proud of herself at that point.

'Tara, listen to me — please. I had nothing to do with it. I had no idea what Grant was up to.'

'Yeah, right,' she scoffed. 'How could you not know? With the amount of money he'd been spending? Fancy cars, fancy houses, expensive holidays . . . Oh yes, I read it all, every word.'

'I've asked myself that hundreds of times, Tara, but I didn't know. Truly I didn't. He told me he was making so much money that he could afford it all and more — and I'm sorry to say I believed him. If I could go back and change it all, I would, in a heartbeat. You must believe me.'

'Okay.' Tara narrowed her eyes. 'So do it, then.'

'How? How can I change things now?'

'For starters, you can pay my grand-dad all the money your husband stole. Then you can repay everyone else.'

'I can't do that,' Petra cried. 'The police seized all the money they could find. I was left with virtually nothing. I lost the house, and practically all I possessed. Believe me, if I could pay, I would.'

'Yeah, well, it's easy to say that now. So I'm going to do what the police can't, what I promised in my emails. I'm going to have revenge, retribution, for Gran and Granddad, as well as everyone else who has lost out.'

As she finished speaking, she thrust a hand into the bag and pulled out a knife. A long-bladed carving knife.

'Tara,' Petra cried, terror striking at the very heart of her. 'Put that away.'

'No. I'm going to put an end to it. People like you and your husband

351

shouldn't be allowed to live. You're no better than common thieves. You've destroyed people's lives. Your husband's already dead, so now it's your turn. You can't pay, but you can die.'

Kelly had been standing just behind Petra, motionless; but now, crouching low, she inched forward towards Tara. 'No, Kelly,' Petra shouted. 'No.' Good God, Tara would kill her pet if she made a further move towards her. She had no doubt about that. A terrible madness blazed in the girl's eyes. 'Sit, Kelly. Sit.'

Kelly did so, but she began to bark loudly. For the first time, Petra wished she had neighbours, someone — anyone — could hear the commotion and suspect that something might be wrong. But there was no one. She was on her own.

Tara started walking towards her, the knife held out in front of her, its sharp blade aimed directly at Petra's chest. Petra put out a hand defensively in front of herself. 'Tara, don't. You don't want to become a murderer. To be sent to some sort of prison.'

'I won't be. No one will suspect it was me. Just as no one knows how — how I've had to support my gran, my mum, and now my granddad.' Her voice broke as her eyes shone with tears. She dashed them away.

Those few seconds, as brief as they were, gave Petra time to grab a cushion from the settee and hold it out in front of her chest. It would afford her some protection, at least. Tara moved closer, her intention evident. Kelly was barking crazily by now, jumping up and down on the spot.

Tara jabbed at Petra, the knife piercing the cushion. A few feathers flew out, spiralling through the air to land soundlessly on the floor.

'Tara, please stop.' Petra's breath came in spurts and gasps from between her parted lips. Tara tried again, jabbing the knife forward repeatedly. A storm of feathers erupted this time. They fluttered down to lie scattered around

Petra's feet like flakes of snow. 'I've done nothing. Please, believe me.'

All of a sudden, Kelly leapt straight at Tara. But Tara was prepared. She lunged forward and struck Kelly in the chest with the knife.

'Kelly,' Petra screamed.

The dog fell to the floor, blood oozing from the wound that Tara had inflicted. Petra started towards her, desperate to hold her pet, to staunch the bleeding, to reassure her.

'Don't move,' Tara warned. 'Stay right where you are.'

'Please, let me help her — at least get a towel to soak up the blood.'

'No. Stay back. You're both going to die. That's justice in its truest form.' She nudged Kelly hard with one foot. Kelly yelped in pain.

Petra ignored Tara's warning and ran to Kelly, dropping to her knees by the side of her. 'Kelly,' she wept. She looked up at Tara then and screamed, 'What's she ever done to you?' She got to her feet and went towards the girl, fully prepared to risk her own life and take her on.

'Petra, stop — right where you are. Don't go any closer.'

Petra swung, unable to believe what she was hearing. It was Finn. He'd let himself in.

17

'Finn,' Petra sobbed. 'It's Kelly. She's hurt. Tara's stabbed her.'

Finn whirled to look at the girl, his expression the blackest, the grimmest, Petra had ever seen it. 'Stand back. Now.'

And amazingly, Tara did, her look one of fear rather than menace.

'Now, drop the knife.'

Again, Tara did as Finn ordered. Finn immediately kicked the weapon into the opposite corner of the room before going to Kelly and dropping to his knees at her side. Tara, every vestige of anger and fight gone from her, collapsed onto the nearest chair and was weeping quietly.

'Petra, dial 999. Get the police. This stops now. I presume it was Tara behind everything?'

'Yes,' Petra softly said. 'She's broken-hearted about her grandfather and wants revenge. He lost a lot of his pension, as well as his job, thanks to Grant; he's suffered a complete breakdown.' She looked meaningfully at Finn. He nodded, clearly understanding all that she didn't say. 'But it's Kelly I'm worried about. She needs help.'

'I'm going to give it to her. Get me a blanket and a towel. Quickly. We need to stop the bleeding and keep her warm.'

Kelly opened her eyes and gazed up at Petra. She gave a small whine as if to say, 'I'll be okay.'

'I'm here, darling. Hold on. I'm calling the vet; you're going to be fine.'

⋆ ⋆ ⋆

And, miraculously, she was.

The police swiftly arrived and when they heard Petra's own story — she told them everything, holding nothing back — and then what Tara had tried to do, they formally cautioned her and led her away. The girl had refused to speak, to

357

explain why she'd done what she had. It was Petra who supplied the details, her name, where she lived, and who her grandparents and mother were. This would practically kill Isobel, Petra decided, on top of everything else she was having to bear. But for the moment, she was much more concerned about Kelly.

Fortunately, the vet quickly arrived and took Kelly back to his surgery, where she'd be kept for a couple of days until he stabilised her.

'Don't worry, Ms Matthews,' he said. 'Mr Hogarth did a splendid job of first aid. The knife wound wasn't too deep. It missed all of her vital organs.'

Once the vet had left with Kelly, Petra collapsed into Finn's arms. She'd wanted to go with Kelly, but Finn had insisted she'd suffered enough trauma for one day and she was to remain at the cottage. The vet had endorsed this, saying, 'It's better if you don't come along. I need to calm Kelly and treat her. She'll need a few stitches and then

I'll sedate her. I'll ring you first thing in the morning and let you know how she is. But you can stop worrying. She's going to be fine.'

'Thank God I came back when I did. I heard the commotion from outside,' Finn said. 'That girl is clearly demented. She needs help. Professional help.'

'Yes. The poor girl's completely traumatised by what's happened to her grandparents.' And she told him exactly what Tara had told her. 'Isobel said a while back that she thought she knew me. It was more than enough to unnerve me. But then, when Judith also thought she knew me — well, neither did much for my piece of mind. Anyway, in the wake of what's happened to Tom and his present mental state, Tara believes it must have been enough to jog a memory, and that's what started Isobel searching through the online newspaper archives. And, of course, she found me. So much for my changed appearance.'

'Well, you can revert back to how you

were. Now the police are involved and know who you really are, the whole story's bound to come out. From what I've heard about her and her propensity for gossiping, I can't imagine Isobel Pearce staying quiet for long.'

'I think she's had enough on her plate with Tom, without gossiping about me. I feel sorry for her. I wish there was something I could do to help her, but I doubt she'd take that from me.'

Finn's expression softened then. 'Look, the Cornish on the whole are very generous, forgiving people, and particularly in Poltreath. You'll be a five-minute wonder, and then it will all blow over. And you'll have me — and my family — to support you. You won't be alone, Petra. Not this time; not anymore.'

'No.' At least she had that to be thankful for.

'Now, how about a drink? I know I need one.'

'You need one?' she echoed. 'I'm

desperate.' She flopped down onto the settee.

Finn opened one of the bottles of wine that she had bought to go with their meal and filled a glass which he then handed to her. He poured himself one and joined her on the settee.

He took a large mouthful and turned to her, his expression belatedly one of anguish. 'I don't know what I'd have done if any harm had come to you. Tara could have killed you . . . ' His voice wavered and broke. He put his glass down and buried his face in his hands.

Petra set her own glass down alongside his and put her arms around him. 'Nothing did happen,' she softly told him. 'Not to me, at any rate. But if you hadn't arrived when you did . . . Oh, Finn, I love you so much.'

He raised his head, his eyes so dark they were almost black. 'I'm never going to let you go, you know. You're stuck with me now.'

'Thank goodness. I don't want to be alone anymore. I want to be with you.'

Finn cupped her face with his two hands and captured her lips with his, gently pushing her back into the cushions, deepening the kiss, until she felt as if they had melted into one.

He suddenly jerked away from her. She stared at him, mystified. He gave a rueful smile.

'If we don't stop now, I can't answer for the consequences, and you've been so sick.'

'You don't need to worry about that. I'm quite recovered.' She reached out for him again. 'I want you, I need you, you'll never know how much,' she groaned.

But he continued to hold her away from him. 'There's something I want to say first — well, ask you.' A flush unexpectedly stained his face.

She stared at him, her heart hammering in her chest. 'O-kay.'

'Will you marry me? I know it's all happened a bit fast, but I also know I can't live without you. I've waited so long for love. And what's just happened has convinced me we mustn't waste a minute more of our lives.'

'Yes, yes, I will. I'll marry you. I don't want to live without you either. But . . . ' She saw him flinch, as if expecting bad news of some sort, a drawback to their plans. 'But I want you to be absolutely sure.'

'I am sure. I've never been more sure of anything in my life.'

'You need to be, because as you've just said, the story's bound to make all the papers again, and this time you'll be caught up in it. Your name could be tarnished because of me and what people will think, at least at first. A-And I couldn't bear that.'

'Sweetheart, whatever happens, we'll deal with it, together. I promise.'

'Really?'

'Yes. As I've already said, Cornish people are amazingly generous, and kind.'

'Well, you say that, but Isobel has been very hostile to me, even before she found my story online. And Marcus hasn't been very friendly.' She peeked up at Finn through lowered lashes. 'He asked me out and I turned him down. I think it irreparably wounded his pride.'

'It probably did.' He mustered a grin as he spoke; a shaky grin, it was true. 'Anyway, enough about them. You rent this cottage, don't you?'

She nodded, wondering what was coming now. However, the phone rang at that point, and Petra reached for it. It was the vet to assure her that his treatment of Kelly had been a total success and she was now sleeping.

'So you can relax, but I'd like to keep her here for forty-eight hours — just to make sure she's okay. But do come and see her in the morning.'

With that worry put to rest, Petra swung back to Finn. 'Kelly's fine.'

'Good. So, what I was going to suggest was that you terminate the rental agreement on this place and move in with me. It'll give us the opportunity and the time to really know each other.'

She smiled at him. 'I'd love to.'

'Really?'

She nodded and he dropped a kiss onto her nose. 'Can we go to bed now, then?'

'What about dinner?' She feigned indignation.

'Who needs dinner? It'll keep till tomorrow, won't it?'

'It certainly will.'

He got to his feet and held out a hand to her. 'Good, because I can't wait any longer. I desperately need to make love to you. I have done since the moment I first set eyes on you.'

They climbed the stairs together, and what followed took Petra's breath away. No man had ever made love to her like Finn did that evening. His tender caresses thrilled every fibre of her being, as his hands and his lips hungrily explored every inch of her.

Petra did manage to ask at one point, slightly nervously, 'What will your parents say about us?'

'Hooray. Finn's finally found his soul mate. Now, stop talking.'

* * *

The following morning, leaving Finn to make some business calls, she decided to go into town and visit Debs and Jenny on her way to see Kelly. She needed to tell them both the truth about herself before the news got out, which it swiftly would.

She went to the gallery first, her heart thumping with dread. How would Debs react? But she needn't have worried. Debs was marvellous. Petra held nothing back; she told her everything and Debs believed her — just as Finn had. She made no mention of Tara's attack upon her and Kelly. The story would leak out soon enough.

'You poor, poor thing,' Debs said, before enfolding Petra in her arms.

Her next stop was Jenny. Again, her story poured from her. Jenny didn't immediately speak; she simply regarded Petra in absolute astonishment. Then, 'Wow! Mind you,' she went on, 'I did think I'd seen you somewhere before.'

'I-I couldn't tell you. I couldn't tell anyone. I'm sorry.'

'Don't be. I'm just glad you felt you could tell me now.'

'Are you okay with it? You believe me?'

'Course I do. I've got to know you well enough now to be sure there's no way you're a fraudster.'

In the wake of her two friends' total understanding, she decided to visit Elizabeth as well. She needn't have worried. The same thing happened with Elizabeth. As soon as Petra finished talking, Elizabeth pulled her into her arms. 'Oh, Petra, you poor darling. How terrible for you. I'm so sorry. But you're family now.' She grinned mischievously. 'Yes, Finn's been here and told us the good news. We'll soon put to rights anyone who speaks against you.'

Petra couldn't recall when she'd last felt so happy, so secure. Protected, even.

And then that evening, to complete her happiness, her mother rang. 'Can we come and stay? We've missed you so much, darling, and we're so sorry for the way we've behaved. Can you ever forgive us?'

'Oh, Mum. Of course I can.'

She replaced the receiver once dates were arranged and swung to look at Finn, who was staying with her, helping her pack up for her move to the manor. 'My parents are coming to stay. As you probably heard, I didn't mention that I'm going to be moving in with you. Shall I stay here until afterwards?' She regarded the boxes they'd already packed. They'd have to be emptied once more.

'Certainly not. Ring your mother back and tell her about us; then tell her she and your father will be very welcome at the manor. Your brother too. Unless . . . ' He also looked unsure at that point. 'Unless you'd rather stay here?' He glanced around the room. 'It is a bit small, though, for four of you.'

'No, I wouldn't rather stay here. I'll ring her now.' She regarded him doubtfully. 'But I'm not sure my brother will want to come.'

Her mother sounded surprised at the news that her daughter was moving in with the man she planned to marry, but she quickly recovered and expressed her delight. 'I can't wait to meet him. Your father will feel the same. I'll ring Paul right now. I'm sure he'll agree to come. He's recently been feeling bad about it all, too.'

'It's all fine,' she told Finn. 'They can't wait to meet you. She thinks my brother will come, too.'

'Thank heavens. Now, come here.'

He held out his arms to her. She moved into them. 'I love you,' she murmured as he captured her lips with his.

'I love you, too. More than I can ever put into words.'

And, not surprisingly, they were the last words either of them spoke for some considerable time, as he demonstrated exactly how much he loved her.